AN EMILIA LONG MYSTERY

SECRETS

IN THE

WOODS

J.E. Smythe

Secrets in the Woods

Copyright © 2017 J.E. Smythe

LEG books may be ordered through booksellers or by Contacting

Lady Esquire Group, LLC
P.O. Box 790672
Charlotte, North Carolina 28206
www.writeleg.com
1-888-988-4249

Because of the dynamic nature of the Internet, any web addresses or links contained in this book may have changed since publication and may no longer be valid. The views expressed in this work are solely those of the author and do not necessarily reflect the views of the publisher, and the publisher hereby disclaims any responsibility for them.

Soft Cover: 978-0-9979175-2-9

EBook: 978-0-9979175-3-6

Part I

1

The dark garage parking lot was dimly lit by a flashing light fixture above the wall. The concrete floor echoed with footsteps of those who made their way to their cars. Emilia Long stood in the shadows checking the time on her cell phone. She leaned against the cold cement wall and folded her arms in nervous anticipation.

She then heard the sound of heels clunking against the concrete floor of the garage. She peeked out from the shadows and waved over a tall blond woman who was dressed in a neatly tailored skirt suit. Emilia had been in communication with the woman for some time. She was on the brink of breaking a national story against one of the wealthiest men in the state of New York. The woman was the wealthy man's Executive Assistant and mistress. She was the only one who could give Emilia what she needed to break the story.

As an Investigative Reporter, Emilia had broken many news stories, but this was going to be the biggest. She'd hope that the woman hadn't changed her mind and had brought with her all the documents that Emilia needed to write her story.

The woman approached Emilia holding a briefcase in her hand. Emilia smiled at her but could see the uncertainty on the woman's face.

"I'm glad you came," Emilia said to the woman.

"Well, I almost didn't," the woman replied.

She opened her briefcase and pulled out a large file. She hesitantly handed it over to Emilia.

"Everything you need is in there," the woman said.

"Thank you so much for this. What are you going to do now?" Emilia replied with gratitude.

"I told him that my mother was sick, so I was taking a leave of absence. When this hits, it's probably going to be an indefinite leave of absence," the woman said.

"I promise, I won't use your name. I don't want this to disturb your life. He never has to know that this came from you," Emilia told her.

"My life has been disturbed for a long time. I've just been in denial about it," the woman said.

"What do you mean?" Emilia asked.

"Is this going to be part of your story?" the woman responded.

"Absolutely not. It's strictly off the record. Besides, it looks like you need someone to talk to," Emilia said.

"I'm from a small town in Maine. It's beautiful there. The water, the air, you can't imagine anything more peaceful. As I look back now, I'm not sure why I ever left. I guess I was chasing something. Anyway, I came to New York for college and never looked back. I barely called home," the woman explained.

"Home is always there. At least that's what I hear," Emilia said.

"That's what I hear too. So, I'm finally going back. It's time for me to figure myself out," the woman said.

"I hope you do," Emilia replied.

"Yeah, I hope so too," the woman said.

The woman gave Emilia a half smile and then walked away. Emilia got into her car and started looking through the files the woman had given her. She quickly stopped as the woman's words about figuring herself out rang in her ear.

Emilia had lived her entire life in New York, but it always felt like she was supposed to be someplace else. Emilia didn't know where that someplace was. She was adopted and had no knowledge of her birth parents, no knowledge of herself. Her adopted mother had died a few years back, and all Emilia had left was her adopted sister Chanel.

Since they were kids, she and Chanel always talked about finding their biological parents one day, but only Chanel actually went through with it. It was a big disappointment for Chanel. She found a mother who was heavily on drugs and had no clue who Chanel's father was.

After that, Emilia decided not to make finding her biological family a priority in her life. She had lived with the feeling of being abandoned her whole life and had learned to deal with it. She'd focused on her career. Of course, every now and then she would wonder what her mother was like and why she chose to give her up. However, she never allowed a random thought to become an overwhelming curiosity.

Emilia laid the file on her passage seat and drove out of the garage into the night air. In order to cover her tracks, she had rented a car and was now on her way to return it. She caught a cab home after turning the car in. The cab ride gave Emilia time to look over the file the woman had given her. But her mind wouldn't allow her to focus on the words on the page.

She had suppressed thoughts of where she came from for so long, and now it seemed to be coming back like a tidal wave. The thoughts always left Emilia empty and feeling like a scared little girl. From what she was told, she had been left at a hospital a few days after she was born. She was fortunate enough that the first foster parent she had adopted her. She never knew what it was like to be bounced around from foster home to foster home.

Her adopted mother didn't have a lot of money, but she took care of her and Chanel and loved them as if they were her own. For that Emilia was grateful.

Emilia walked into her dark apartment with the glimmering lights of the TV shining throughout the room. Her longtime boyfriend, Donavan, laid on the sofa asleep. Emilia had met Donavan while they were in college. They were only friends for a long time. After college, Donavan left for law school, and Emilia started interning at a small newspaper in the city.

Emilia had never been the kind of girl who got caught up in a guy. But when she ran into Donavan years later, there was just something about him. His patience with her won her heart. Most guys she dated never made the effort to break down the wall that Emilia had built. But Donavan knew that wall was from a place of hurt. Emilia tried to give Donavan her whole heart, but she knew that so much of it had been broken that there just wasn't much of it to give. So she tried to give Donavan as much of her as possible. She wondered how long it would be before that wasn't enough for him.

She walked over to the sofa and woke Donavan up. "Come on, go to bed," she said to him.

"Oh, you're home," he replied.

"Yeah. Were you waiting up?" she asked.

"Like always," he said with a smile. "Did you get what you need?"

"Yup, like always," Emilia responded not giving him a smile back.

"You don't seem too happy about it," Donavan said.

"I'm about to destroy someone's life. No matter how despicable they are, it's not an easy thing to do," Emilia replied.

Donavan reached over to Emilia and begun rubbing her shoulders. The gestured relaxed Emilia a bit, and she fell into his arms. Donavan held her tightly as they laid back on the sofa.

2

The sun came up and brightened the downtown Manhattan sky. Emilia rolled over in her bed allowing her long dark hair to fling across the pillow. She stretched her toned arms and placed them across Donavan's chest. The feel of her skin against his awoken Donavan just long enough to allow him to begin gently stroking her arm. Donavan's gentle caress comforted Emilia as she let out a soft sigh and dozed back to sleep.

As they laid there, they heard the front door slam shut, and then a loud voice yelled, "Emilia!" "Em… where are you?!"

"Really?" Donavan moaned.

Just then, their bedroom door opened and Chanel stood in the doorway.

"Are you really still in bed?" Chanel said to Emilia. "Oh. Hey Donavan."

Chanel liked Donavan for her sister. She thought he was a good man and really loved her sister. But a piece of her felt that she had to be tough on Donavan from time to time just to make sure he did right by Emilia. Under all of Emilia's tough exterior was a vulnerability that could be crushed with the slightest heartbreak and Chanel knew that.

"Good Morning Chanel," Donavan answered in an annoyed tone.

"Well, good morning to you too," Chanel replied.

"What time is it?" Emilia asked.

"Time for you to get up. We have plans remember?" Chanel replied.

"Ok just wait for me in the living room I'm coming," Emilia said.

"Alright. But hurry up," Chanel said, "bye Donavan."

"Bye Chanel," Donavan replied still feeling annoyed.

Donavan rolled over and moaned, "Why does she have a key to your apartment again?"

"Because she's my sister," Emilia answered while getting out of the bed and heading to the bathroom.

"A sister who has no boundaries," Donavan said under his breath while turning around in the bed one more time.

Emilia quickly got ready and gave Donavan a goodbye kiss. She ran into the living to meet Chanel who was snooping through Donavan's jacket pockets.

"What are you doing?!" Emilia yelled in a whisper as she was closing the bedroom door behind her.

Chanel had a nosey side to her. She was the only artist that Emilia knew who also had every kind of computer spyware. Chanel could hack into any system she wanted to. Emilia always warned her to be careful but Chanel somehow got great thrills from it. Emilia benefited from Chanel's talents as well, especially when she wanted to get more information on someone she's writing a story on and couldn't find anyone willing to talk.

"You know what I always say. Trust but verify," Chanel replied as she pushed Donavan's jacket away from her. "What I really want to do is get my hands on his pants' pocket. You think you can go back into the room and get it for me?"

"No… what you really want to do is get up so we can go," Emilia said as she grabbed hold of Chanel's arm and pushed her through the door.

Emilia followed Chanel to an old junkyard in Brooklyn. They walked through rusted and abandoned metal materials. Emilia drank her coffee as she watched Chanel dive into what Emilia believed to be nothing but trash.

"Did you really wake me up early this morning to play in trash?" Emilia asked.

"This is not trash sister. This is art," Chanel replied.

"Where do you see the art?" Emilia responded as she looked around in discuss.

"It's all around you. You, my dear Emilia, have no imagination. You never had," Chanel said.

"Chanel. This is trash, and I'm starting to worry about you," Emilia said.

"Yes!" Chanel yelled as she pulled out a long indescribable metal object from the bottom of the pile.

"Yes what? What the hell is that Chanel?" Emilia asked.

"This is what I've been looking for," Chanel answered.

"And that is?" Emilia asked again.

"My next sculptor. My masterpiece," Chanel replied with stars in her eyes.

Emilia looked at the big object in her sister's hand and then back at Chanel. "Ok, it's official. You have lost your mind," Emilia said. "I always thought this day would come."

"Will you leave me alone Emilia. This is art. You can't see it because you are not creative. Ma always said if you want to discover the beauty in something, look at it from all angles," Chanel said.

"Things are more than what they seem," both Emilia and Chanel said together with a chuckle as they remembered their adopted mother's words.

"Right. Now help me get this back to my studio," Chanel said.

"I'm not touching that thing," Emilia replied.

"Really Emilia? You're not going to help me," Chanel said.

"That thing is dusty and rusted. And, is that mold?" Emilia said.

"You know you're getting to be a little bit uptight," Chanel replied.

"I don't care what you say about me. I'm not touching that thing," Emilia responded.

"Fine. My studio is just two blocks away anyway. I'll take it myself," Chanel said as she began to drag the object behind her.

Emilia followed closely behind as she chuckled to herself. The sight of Chanel, in her long flowy black skirt and multi-color loose fitted top with the matching head wrap, dragging an old rusted piece of metal down the Brooklyn streets amused Emilia.

When they reached the building Chanel's studio was in, they got to the stairs, and Emilia watched for a moment as Chanel tried to pull the object up the stairs.

"Oh for Christ sake," Emilia said. She threw away her coffee, took off the scarf that was around her neck and wrapped it around her hands. Then she picked up the other end of the object and helped Chanel carry it into her studio.

Chanel studio was a huge open warehouse. One side of it was set up for living space, and the other side was filled with her artwork and art supplies. She and Emilia set the object down next to her workbench, and Emilia took a seat next to the workbench and watched as her sister twisted the object from side to side with pure joy in her eyes.

"You're not seriously going to work with that thing, are you?" Emilia said.

"Yes I am," Chanel replied.

Emilia shook her head and smiled at the satisfactory look on her sister's face. Chanel's zeal for life always amazed Emilia. She wished she could live her life with such optimism. Chanel was the one who always kept their house filled with excitement and laughter as they were growing up. Emilia needed that. She needed to smile.

"Why are you just sitting there?" Chanel asked.

"What else am I supposed to be doing?" asked Emilia as she got up to walk around.

"Oh, I know what's going on with you," Chanel said with a slight smile.

"What?" Emilia asked curiously.

"Your birthday is coming up, and you always act weird around your birthday," Chanel replied.

"I do not act weird around my birthday," replied Emilia, "I just hate it when you plan things that I don't want to do."

"I plan fun things for your birthdays," Chanel said.

"No, you don't. All I want to do for my birthday is stay home and relax," Emilia said. "It's the same thing I always want to do every year. But somehow you seem to look over that and plan something anyway."

"Just because you're boring does not mean that I, your loving sister, have to let you stay that way," Chanel said.

"Chanel, listen to me very closely. Do. Not. Plan. Anything. For my birthday," Emilia emphasized.

"I make no such promises," Chanel said.

"Oh God," Emilia moaned under her breath and then hopelessly sat on the sofa.

It wasn't that Emilia hated getting old, it was that she just hated being reminded of the day she was abandoned outside a Brooklyn hospital with nothing but an old blanket wrapped around her. That was not a day she chose to celebrate.

Chanel walked over to Emilia and sat down across from her.

"You need to start appreciating who you are Em," Chanel said.

"What are you talking about?" Emilia asked.

"You have a whole lot of unanswered questions," Chanel said. Then she looked over at a big chest that sat in the corner of her living room.

Emilia looked in that same direction and then a panic came over her.

"No, I'm not… I'm not looking in there," she replied.

"Em. Ma did right by us and got some information about our families. She knew that the day would come when we would want it," Chanel said.

"That day hasn't come for me," Emilia said.

"It helped me to find out Em," Chanel said.

"What are you talking about? You didn't get out of bed for days," Emilia replied.

"But when I did get out of bed, I was a better person because I now know," Chanel explained.

"Well, I'm not ready," Emilia said.

"Don't you want to know who you are?" Chanel asked.

"I know who I am," Emilia said.

Every birthday, Chanel tried to get Emilia to open the chest, and every birthday Emilia would decline. Finding out about her birth mother frightened Emilia. It was a road that she just didn't feel like she had to go down.

Emilia gave one final glance at the chest and then shook her head. Her adopted mother told her and Chanel about the chest and warned them that they should be mentally ready before they open the chest, Emilia didn't feel mentally ready. She felt like she had enough information, whoever her birth mother was, she didn't love or want her. That's all she needed to know.

3

After leaving Chanel's studio, Emilia went straight to her office. She wanted to get a jump start on writing her story. Emilia focused all of her attention on her computer screen, making sure to capture everything she had read in the file. She wanted to get her story out before anyone else did.

Emilia's work always came first, it was all about the story. She wasn't afraid to go anywhere and do anything. She was always seeking the truth. Always chasing what it was the people were hiding.

Chanel and Donavan sometimes would worry about the places her searches would lead her. She once broke a story about a gambling ring inside of an upscale night club. She had to meet her informant in a back alley in one of the worst areas in New York. Donavan and Chanel begged her not to go. Donavan even offered to go with her. But Emilia wouldn't hear of it. She had to find the truth and she did. She broke the story and connected the gambling ring to a local politician.

"One of these stories is going to take you out," Chanel would say to her.

That didn't ring true for Emilia. She was driven by what she did. It was always about the next story and the story after that. Nothing deterred her. That was until now. The woman who gave her the files struck a nerve in Emilia with her voice of longing for home and for peace. She couldn't put her finger on why the woman's words continued to whisper in her ear. It was something about the look on her face. It was a look of finally understanding who she was and being satisfied with that person.

Emilia sat back in her chair thinking about that chest. There was such a big chunk of her life that she knew nothing about. She'd always wondered where her olive skin-tone and bone straight long hair came from. Chanel would joke that she must have had Indian in her family or maybe her mother was an Italian immigrant who was scared off by immigration and had to leave her behind. Chanel must have had a million stories about Emilia's birth mother and each one more elaborate than the other.

She seemed more intrigued by Emilia's heritage than Emilia was. At least Emilia tried her best not to let on that she was curious. Chanel romanticized Emilia's birth but Emilia knew better. She was sure her birth mother must have left her because of something as simple as not being able to take care of her for whatever reason, but it also could be that her birth mother was on drugs like Chanel's birth mother or a prostitute, or maybe she just didn't want to be her mother. Emilia had convinced herself a long time ago that not knowing was what was best for her and she intended on sticking to that.

As Emilia tried to pull herself together and go back to work, there was a soft knock at the door and her boss, Christina, walked in. Christina was an older lady who had been in the news industry for a very long time. Emilia looked up to Christina and valued her opinion. Christina was the one who took Emilia out of the internship world and gave her the first story that launched her career. Christina was now her editor, and she always strived to make Christina proud.

"How's it going?" Christina asked.

"Trying to organize all this information that I got," Emilia replied.

"So you're still going through with that story?" Christina asked again.

"Absolutely," Emilia said, "why wouldn't I?"

"Don't you ever want to do a story with a little more heart Emilia?" Christina asked again.

"What do you mean more heart?" Emilia replied.

"I don't know. Something that intrigues our readers. That will pull at their heart string. Something that they can connect to," Christina explained.

"I'm not sure what you mean," Emilia said.

"Well, take this story for instance. What would make a man who has everything do what he did?" Christina said.

"Greed," Emilia replied.

"Yes, that's true," Christina said. "But he has a life, kids, and a wife. Did you even talk to the wife or did you go straight for the mistress? Did you consider how she's feeling? As a married woman, I can tell you the wife knows a hell of a lot more than what she says."

"I didn't consider that," Emilia said.

"Because you always miss the family angle. That's the heart of the story," Christina said.

"That's not what I do Chris. I'm an investigative reporter, not some neighborhood reporter discussing the cherry blossoms and damn windmills," Emilia said.

"I'm not asking you to do that Emilia. I just want you to be willing to expand yourself a bit. What's wrong with that?" Christina replied.

"There's nothing wrong with that Chris. But it's not what I do. The stories I've written have kept this newspaper at number one for about a year now," Emilia told her, "why would you want me to change that?"

"As your editor, I don't. As your friend, I can see that there's something more inside of you that you are fighting hard not to let out. Something is eating away at you," Christina responded.

"Now you sound like Chanel. So I'll tell you like I told her, I'm fine," Emilia said.

"Ok, you're fine. Just remember that the best writing comes from a real place. You have an incredible story inside of you," Christina said. "Don't you think it's time you stop running from it?"

Christina walked out of Emilia's office leaving Emilia to ponder all that she had said. Emilia sat back in her chair looking out of the window. She had grown tired of people constantly telling her to face whatever it was that was inside of her. She didn't want to; she wasn't ready. She liked the way her life was, just the way it was, and she had no intention of disturbing or interrupting that.

4

A few days had gone by, and Emilia's story had come out causing a full-on media frenzy. Emilia sat in her office watching the news coverage of the subject of her story being lead out of his home in handcuffs. She felt like she should be celebrating, but she wasn't quite in the mood. It was her birthday, and like most of her birthdays, she just wanted the day to pass without any fanfare. She was praying that Chanel didn't try to surprise her with anything.

She'd had Donavan pretty well trained that he may sneak her a rose or a card but he didn't mention her birthday. The first year they were together, Emilia was in her office and Donavan had somehow found out it was her birthday. He thought it would be a great gesture to come to her office with a large teddy bear that sang Stevie Wonder's version of

Happy Birthday. Emilia got enraged. Everyone in her office was staring and the day that Emilia had hoped would just go away, was becoming a big event. She yelled at Donavan, threw the teddy bear on the floor, and stormed out of the office. She didn't talk to Donavan for almost an entire month, no matter how hard he tried to apologize.

Through the years, Donavan stayed clear of her birthday. He didn't make any more big gestures and only said happy birthday after he gauged her mood. It wasn't any different this morning when they woke up. Donavan said good morning and gave her a kiss. After she smiled and said good morning back, he cautiously told her happy birthday. Emilia said thank you and then walked away. She then found herself standing in the bathroom fighting back tears. Her birthday was a constant reminder that she was unwanted and unloved by the people who were supposed to love her the most.

As she sat at her desk, she was still trying to fight off the emotion of the day. She wondered if Chanel was right. Did she need answers about where she came from so that she could stop the slow torturing of her soul? She began to think that maybe if she knew why she was abandoned, then maybe somehow her birthday wouldn't affect her as much. The thought was still burning in her head when her office door opened, and Chanel slowly walked in holding a cupcake and quietly singing happy birthday.

"Chanel," Emilia moaned.

"Happy Birthday dear Emilia. Happy Birthday to you," Chanel sang. "Now blow out the candle.

Emilia just looked at her sternly.

"Fine. I blow it out myself," Chanel replied.

After she blew out the candle, she sat it down in front of Emilia. "At least eat the cupcake, it's red velvet."

Emilia picked up the cupcake and begun to nibble on it. It was delicious. She licked the icing and licked her lips as she savored the taste.

"So, what are we doing later tonight?" Chanel asked with a giggle.

"Chanel!" Emilia said with a full mouth of cupcake.

"Calm down I was just joking," Chanel proclaimed. "Anyway, I have to go. Just wanted to bring my favorite sister her birthday cupcake."

"I'm your only sister and thank you," Emilia said with a slight satisfactory smile.

Later that evening when Emilia got home, there was an eerie calm in the air. She walked up to the front door of her apartment and opened it. Her apartment was dimly lit with candles, and soft music was playing in the background. The room was filled with red roses, and the floor was covered in red rose peddles.

Emilia closed the door behind her and slowly walked into the living room. Her heart was pounding a mile a minute because she just knew that Donavan was trying to celebrate her birthday.

"Donavan!" Emilia called out.

Donavan emerged from the kitchen dressed in a tuxedo and carrying a silver tray. He looked at Emilia with love in his eyes but all Emilia could see was her own anger at what he had done.

"What is this?" she asked.

"Something…" Donavan began to say.

"It better not be for my birthday," Emilia said angrily.

"No. This is for something else," Donavan said.

"What?" Emilia asked.

Donavan walked up to her and sat the silver covered tray down on the table beside them. He grabbed hold of her hands and said, "I want this day to be filled with memory of love for you. I want you to forever look on the calendar knowing this day is coming and smile because your heart is filled with joy."

"How do you see that happening?" Emilia asked.

Donavan reached to the silver covered tray and uncovered it. On the tray laid a small black box. Donavan took the box in his hand and then dropped to his knees.

"Emilia, I loved you from the moment I saw you. I knew that there was no other woman for me, you were the one. I want to love you for the rest of my life. Will you marry me?"

Emilia's eyes got glossy. The room started to spin. No words could come out of her mouth. Her heart was beating a mile a minute and she could hardly catch her breath.

"I…" Emilia started to say and tried to take one quick deep breath. "I got to go."

Emilia ran out of the apartment and didn't stop running until she was half way down the street. She looked back at her apartment building and wanted to go back and apologize to Donavan, but she couldn't bring herself to do it. She had to go. She had to be away from him.

5

Emilia found herself outside of Chanel's studio. She began to pound the door as hard as she could. Chanel hastily opened it dressed in a dashiki gown and a head wrap. She looked shocked to see Emilia standing there.

Emilia walked into Chanel's studio to the smell of incense and the sound of soft jazz playing in the background.

"Do you have a guest?" Emilia asked looking around.

"No. I'm setting the ambiance for my creativity," Chanel replied. "What are you doing here?"

"Chanel, you are not going to believe this," Emilia began to explain. "Donavan proposed."

"Again, what are you doing here?" Chanel asked as she turned the music off.

"What do you mean? Did you hear what I said?" Emilia asked. "Donavan proposed. Tonight. Like ten minutes ago."

Chanel looked at Emilia perplexed and waited for her to explain further why she was not at home with Donavan. But Chanel's unaffected reaction bewildered Emilia. "Why isn't this surprising you?" Emilia asked.

"What do you want me to say?" Chanel replied.

"I want you to be as shocked as I am," Emilia said. "I mean he had the room filled with roses and candles and music and the ring…"

"Hey, what was wrong with the ring? That was good quality ring," Chanel proclaimed.

"I knew it! You were in on this," Emilia said.

"Ok so I was. But so what?" Chanel replied.

"So what? Chanel I said I didn't want anything for my birthday and you end up helping my boyfriend plan a proposal," explained Emilia.

"See that's where you're wrong. It was more about the proposal than your birthday. If you think about it, it was a proposal that happened to be on your birthday and you said nothing about not wanting a proposal," Chanel said.

"Chanel," Emilia groaned while shaking her head.

"Chanel nothing. Just calm down and tell me what happened," she said to Emilia

"Nothing happened because I left," Emilia replied.

"You left?! What do you mean you left?" Chanel asked.

"Just what I said. He asked and I left," Emilia answered.

"Wait… wait. Don't tell me you left that man on his knees."

"Well…."

"Oh my God Emilia. Are you serious?"

"What was I supposed to do?"

"Answer his question."

"I didn't have an answer Chanel. I didn't know what to say."

"Wow. You're more messed up than I thought."

"You know what, this isn't the time for your jokes."

"I'm not joking Em. You're screwed up."

Chanel looked at Emilia for a moment and then got up and walked over to the trunk. She opened it and pulled out a large folder. She walked back over to Emilia and sat it on her lap and said, "You have to face your demons Em. It's time."

"What is this?" Emilia was afraid to touch the folder.

"Ma had two folders in that trunk. One for me and one for you. I opened mine, this is yours. Open it Em. Whatever is in here has a hold on you so strong that it's starting to destroy you," Chanel explained.

"You're being dramatic," Emilia replied tossing the folder on the table.

"I'm not Em. I've been seeing it since we were kids, but now… you can't even say yes to the man you love, and

I know you love him because I know you. Don't let what's in here make you live your life in misery," Chanel explained.

Chanel took the folder from off the table and placed it in Emilia's hands. She looked at her lovingly then wiped the drop of tear from her eyes. Chanel then got up and left Emilia alone with the folder.

6

The next morning, Emilia woke up on Chanel's sofa with the folder pressed against her chest. She had not worked up the nerves to open it. Emilia sat up and saw Chanel still fast asleep. She went to the bathroom to wash her face. When she came out, Chanel was still asleep. Emilia looked around the room and saw the folder sitting where she left it, on the sofa. She began to walk out of Chanel's studio without the folder, but couldn't. She knew Chanel was right. She had to find out what was in the folder. She had to know where she came from and why she was given away.

Emilia walked over to the sofa and picked up the folder. She gave Chanel's sleeping body a faint smile and walked out of the door. On the way home, she wanted to open the folder but her nervousness wouldn't allow her to.

When she got home, she opened the door and all remanence from the night before was gone. Donavan was sitting on the sofa with his head bowed as if he knew she was coming and he was waiting for her.

Emilia walked over to him and sat next to him silently. She wanted to tell him about the folder in her hands, but Donavan felt distant. His eyes wouldn't lock on her. His body language was cold and removed.

"I'm sorry," Emilia whispered.

But Donavan did not speak. He kept rubbing his hands together like they were in pain. Emilia didn't know what to say or do. She allowed her eyes to move around the room searching for an escape. Then she saw suitcases sitting by the dining room table.

"What… what's going on?" Emilia asked.

"I think it's time Em," Donavan said in a slow, subdued tone.

"Time for what?" Emilia asked.

Donavan looked up and finally locked eyes with her. His face was in pain and his energy was lost.

"I love you more than I can explain. But this, us, it's just getting hard. I don't know how to make you happy. I don't know if you want me to," he told her.

Emilia was at a loss for words. She wanted to tell Donavan how much she appreciated him and how much she did love him. But her words would not form to express her emotions.

Donavan got up and walked over to the dining room table where his suitcases were. He hesitated for a moment and then reached into his pocket. He pulled out the ring box and placed it on the kitchen table.

"This is yours. I bought it for you," Donavan said before picking up his suitcases and walked out of the door.

Emilia stood up and slowly walked over to the dining room table. She gradually rubbed her fingers across the box and began to weep. From the first day she met Donavan, she'd been pushing him away, but he never left. He'd never abandoned her, not until now. Emilia lost the feelings in her legs and fell to the floor. She buried her face in her hands trying to control the tears, but her eyes were soaked. She lifted her face and saw the folder staring back at her daring her to open it. Emilia reached for it, and finally she opened it.

The first thing that popped up at her was a birth certificate. Emilia found a few things odd about this birth certificate, it did not have the name of her birth parents and it was from the state of North Carolina. At first, Emilia thought it didn't belong to her. Then she saw her name, Emilia Elizabeth. But the last name was different, instead of Long, the name was Potter. Her baby footprint and handprint and weight was all on there. That was about it.

Emilia flipped the birth certificate to the other side and saw another piece of folded paper. It looked like a letter. Emilia opened the letter and begun to read it.

To who whom it may concern:
Please take care of this baby. Her name is Emilia Elizabeth.
Shower her with love. Protect her and keep her safe. One
day when she's all grown up tell her that she came from a
small town call Arbor. Tell her that I'm sorry, but she
deserved more than what was waiting for her in Arbor. Tell
her to shine bright. Tell her to smile.

Emilia squeezed the paper tightly in her hands. She just knew it was from her birth mother. She wanted to cry again, but then her eyes landed on newspaper clippings. The first was of a group of cheerleaders in a pyramid formation and one girl at the top of the formation. She read the small print at the bottom of the picture and it said 'Arbor High cheerleaders celebrating the win of the football team with an amazing pyramid. At the top of the pyramid is the captain, Elizabeth, Lizzie, Potter.'

Emilia froze in place. Could this be her mother? The disheveled newspaper cut out was hard to read and the black and white coloring made it even harder to get a good look at the girl's face. Emilia looked at the date at the top of the page and it said 1989. That had to have been one year before she was born. Emilia wondered if the reason why her birth mother gave her up was because she was in high school.

Emilia saw another newspaper clipping. This time the picture was clear. Emilia got lost in memorizing every inch of Elizabeth's face. Her smile, her bone structure, and her perfectly styled hair. Elizabeth was gorgeous. Emilia touched her face to see if she had Elizabeth's features. She smiled to herself. Then she read the article. It said that Elizabeth was missing. Emilia looked at the date, 1990. The month she was said to be missing would put it right at the time she may have discovered she was pregnant.

Emilia dropped the folder on the ground and stood up in a panic state of confusion. She wondered if Elizabeth had run away from Arbor when she discovered she was pregnant and somehow found her way to New York. Then Emilia suddenly stopped pacing and wondered out loud, "Is she still in New York?"

Emilia quickly opened her laptop and tried to search for any Elizabeth Potter in the state of New York. But none of the Elizabeth Potter that she found matched. None was an African American woman in her mid-fifties.

"Maybe she changed her name," Emilia said to herself.

But what could her new name be. Then Emilia looked down at the folder. Her birth certificate came from the state of North Carolina. "Did she go back home? How did I end up at the hospital in Brooklyn?" Emilia asked out loud.

Emilia was lost. Nothing made sense. She was more confused now than ever before. *Who was her Elizabeth, Lizzie, Potter and what was she doing in Brooklyn?*

She took out her cell phone and called Chanel. From the sound of Chanel's voice, Emilia could tell that she was still asleep.

"Chanel wake up I need you," Emilia said.

"For what? What's going on?" Chanel said in a groggy voice.

"I need you to see what you can find on someone named Elizabeth Potter," Emilia told her.

"Who's Elizabeth Potter?" Chanel asked still sounding half asleep.

"I think she's my mother," Emilia said in a low voice.

"Oh my God. You opened the folder," Chanel said, "give me a minute let me get to my computer.

Emilia could hear Chanel typing away on her computer. She grew anxious with every passing second.

"Do you have anything else on her?" Chanel asked,

"Only that her nickname is Lizzie and she's from Arbor, NC," Emilia said.

"Ok," Chanel said as she begun typing again. "Oh my God Em, I think I found her. There's an Elizabeth Potter living in upstate New York. There's no picture of her but it says she was born in Arbor. Do you know how old she may be?"

"Maybe in her forties. If this is my mother, then she may have had me when she was a teenager," Emilia said,

"Well, the age fits. This Elizabeth Potter is forty-three," Chanel said.

"Can you text me the address?" Emilia asked taking a deep breath.

"Yeah I can," Chanel said. "I can be ready in like two seconds and go with you."

"No. I think I need to go by myself," Emilia said.

7

Emilia pulled into the wide driveway of a fancy Charlotte home. She stepped out of her car and looked around. The house was large and gorgeous. The palms of her hand grew sweaty. She may finally come face to face with her mother and that scared her. She wondered if Lizzie would accept her or tell her to get lost. The anticipation formed knots in the pit of her stomach.

She walked up to the front door and rang the bell. Then she stood back and waited patiently. The door opened, and a mildly attractive white woman opened the door. The layers of makeup on her face could not hide the hard life she must have lived.

Emilia's eyes lingered on the woman wondering what her connection was to Lizzie. The woman's body language was detached and defensive.

"May I help you?" the woman asked.

"Hello, I'm looking for Elizabeth Potter," Emilia answered.

"I'm Elizabeth Potter, Well its Henry now. Do I know you?" the woman replied.

"Elizabeth Lizzie Potter?" Emilia asked again suspiciously.

"My name is Elizabeth Potter-Henry. You still haven't told me who you are," the woman said.

Emilia stepped back slightly in shock at the woman before her. She wasn't sure how this person could be Lizzie. She looked nothing like the pictures from the newspaper clippings. Emilia's mind tried to focus but she was confused.

"Ma'am. Who are you?" the woman asked.

"I'm sorry but I was looking for the Elizabeth Potter from Arbor, North Carolina," Emilia said.

She took out her cell phone and tried to pull out the pictures she took of the newspaper clippings. But before she did, she took a quick picture of the woman without her knowing. Then she pulled up the picture of Lizzie and studied it. She looked back up at the woman. Emilia knew that there was no way that those two women could be the same person.

"I think you should leave," the woman said seeming nervous.

"You can't be Elizabeth Potter," Emilia said.

"Please leave now," the woman said sounding almost terrified, then she slammed the door in Emilia's face.

Emilia went back to her car and looked at the picture she took of the woman. She then texted the picture to Chanel who immediately called her.

"Who the hell is this?" Chanel asked.

"Apparently, it's Elizabeth Potter," Emilia said.

"It is?" Chanel asked again.

"No. Something's not right," Emilia said as she started to pull out of the woman's driveway.

"Ok, give me a minute let me run this picture through my new facial recognition software," Chanel said.

"Your what? How do you have these things?" Emilia asked.

"You know better than to question me," Chanel said, "oh wait a minute. I got a match."

"For what?" Emilia asked.

"You're right. Thant's not Elizabeth Potter," Chanel said.

"Who is it?" Emilia asked as she pulled over to the side of the road.

"According to this, it's a woman by the name of Michelle Gilbert and this lady has a long record. I see why she needed a new name," Chanel explained

"So how did she get Lizzies' name and documents?" Emilia asked.

"I have no idea. The facial recognition doesn't tell me all that," Chanel said.

"But I bet she will," Emilia said as she hung up the phone.

Emilia made a quick U-turn and went back to the woman's house. She rang the doorbell repeatedly and banged on the door. The woman opened the door almost in anger.

"What is it now?" she asked.

"How did you become Elizabeth Potter, Michelle?" Emilia asked sternly.

The woman's face was in shock. She looked over her shoulder as if to make sure no one heard what Emilia had just said. Then she walked out on to the porch and closed the door behind her.

"Please don't do this," the woman said.

"If you don't tell me how you got Elizabeth's documents, I'm going to call the cops and blow your life up," Emilia said.

"Ok. I'll tell you what you want to know," the woman said.

"What did you do to the real Elizabeth?" Emilia asked.

"Nothing. I don't even know who that is. I left Florida and was looking for an escape. I ran into this biker gang of sorts. One of them promised me that they could give me face documents for a price. I gave them all the money I had, and they gave me this new name. I promise you, that's all I know. Please don't destroy my life. I can't go back to what I used to be," the woman explained.

"Where did you run into this biker gang?" Emilia asked.

"Some small town. I can't tell you the name," the woman said.

Emilia looked at the woman again and took in her story. The thought of some bikers having Lizzie's personal information bewildered Emilia. She wondered if these bikers had something to do with Randel's death and Lizzie's disappearance.

"Before I leave, did these bikers have a gang name or some way for me to find them?' Emilia asked the woman.

"It was so many years ago, I doubt if they're still around. But they went by the name of Devil's Skull," she said as she walked towards her front door and went in.

The woman gently closed the door behind her leaving Emilia standing on the front porch. Emilia had to find out what happened to those bikers and what they had to do with Elizabeth. On her way home, she texted Chanel. She had to go back to the beginning of where it all started for her and needed Chanel's support.

8

Emilia sat on a wooden bench holding a cup of coffee in her hand dressed in jeans, a t-shirt and short leather jacket. She wore dark sunglasses to hide the puffiness of her eyes from crying. She had gone back to her apartment after meeting with the fake Elizabeth Potter and cried the whole night. Thoughts of the real Elizabeth, her mother, roamed through her mind the entire night. She wondered what she sounded like, did she have a favorite color, book, or TV show. But she mostly thought about what happened to her.

"Why am I meeting you in front of a hospital this early in the morning?" Chanel said as she walked up to Emilia.

Emilia looked up at her through her dark shades, "To get some answers."

"At this hospital?" Chanel asked as she sat down next to her sister.

"Because this may be the only place that I can get some answers," Emilia said.

"Like what?" Chanel asked.

"Like, I was born in Arbor, North Carolina," Emilia answered.

"Yeah so?" Chanel asked again confused.

"So, how did I end up at this hospital in Brooklyn, New York?"

Chanel looked around bewildered. She, like Emilia had always assumed that Emilia's birth mother was somewhere in New York.

"Here, this was in the folder too," Emilia handed Chanel the newspaper clipping with the picture of Lizzie.

Chanel looked at the clipping and smiled, "She's beautiful Em."

"She was in high school when she had me," Emilia said looking far off into the distance.

"Well, that explains why she gave you up. Same thing with my birth mother," Chanel said.

"Yeah, I guess," Emilia replied

"So, what are we going to do?" Chanel asked.

Emilia looked at Chanel. She took off her sunglasses to better connect with Chanel's eyes. "There's more to this story," Emilia said. "There's more to my story, and I have to find out what it is."

Chanel grabbed hold of her sister's hand and replied, "Then let's go."

The two of them walked into the busy Brooklyn hospital and begun to look around. They asked a passing nurse where they could find birth records and information. The Nurse directed them to the administration office.

They found an older lady sitting at the desk, and they walked up to her. Chanel sat down first and then Emilia sat down nervously.

"May I help you?" the woman asked.

"Hi, my name is Emilia Long and several years ago I was left at this hospital as a baby," Emilia explained. "I was wondering if there's any information on who left me.

"We don't tend to keep those type of information ma'am," the woman replied.

Emilia growing frustrated said, "Can you please check."

"Ma'am, I'm sorry but I won't be able to help you," the woman answered.

"You haven't even tried to help me!" Emilia could hear herself starting to yell.

Her normal even and understanding demeanor, which had put most of her informants at ease in the past, was now out of the door and her raw emotions had taken over.

The woman looked to have grown angry. Chanel noticed that the conversation was getting out of hand so she stepped in. "Miss, my sister was left here and she's trying to find her birth mother. Please, any help you can give would help."

The woman looked back and forth at Chanel and Emilia and then started typing on her computer. "What was your name again?"

"Emilia Long."

"Sorry nothing came up for an Emilia Long," the woman said.

"What about Elizabeth Potter or Emilia Potter?" Emilia added

"Sorry, nothing," the woman said again.

"Do you remember anyone talking about a baby being left at this hospital twenty-seven years ago or maybe you remember something, even something small?" Emilia asked.

"I've only been working here for five years, and I haven't heard about a baby that was left here twenty-seven years ago," the woman said. She then looked at the disappointed faces on Chanel and Emilia and thought for a moment.

"There is one person who may know. She's been working here for about thirty years as a nurse," the woman said.

"Who is it? Is she on duty now?" Emilia said.

The woman's face turned sad, "no, she's not on duty, but she is in the hospital."

"Where?" Emilia asked again.

"Her husband is here in ICU. He's dying from cancer," the woman replied.

Emilia looked at Chanel wondering if she should bother who ever this nurse was. But she had to know if the nurse knew anything.

"Please, I promise I won't stress her out but I just have to talk to her," Emilia pleaded.

The woman thought for a moment, "Ok, she's upstairs room 801, her name is Catharine Jones. But don't tell anyone I told you this."

"Thank you," Emilia said as she and Chanel got up and rushed out of the office.

The elevator ride up to the 8th floor was quiet. The only sound Emilia could hear was the sound of her heart pounding a mile a minute. She had all her hopes on this moment. As soon as the elevator door opened, Emilia and Chanel ran out to quickly find room 801. They stood outside the room and couldn't bring themselves to go in.

"May I help you?" a woman's voice called from behind them.

Chanel and Emilia turned around to find a petite older black woman standing there with confusion in her eyes.

"Hi. We're looking for Ms. Catherine Jones," Emilia said.

"I'm Catherine Jones. Do I know you?" she replied.

"Um… here," Emilia reached into her pocket and pulled out one of her business cards. She thought that showing the woman that she was a reporter may help this moment feel less awkward.

Catherine took the business card and looked at it seeming even more confused. "Why is a reporter looking for me?" Catherine asked.

"Um… I wanted to ask you some questions about something that happened a few years ago," Emilia said reverting to her reporter tone.

Catherine looked at the card again and then back at Emilia. She stared at Emilia for a moment and then smiled. "You're Emilia?" Catherine asked.

"Yes. Do you know me, I mean do you remember me?" Emilia asked dropping her reporter tone for a rush of eagerness.

Catherine sat down on a nearby chair and smiled up at Emilia. Chanel grabbed hold of Emilia's hand and squeezed it tightly. They both had a sense that Catherine knew something about Emilia, maybe even something about Elizabeth.

"I was the one who found you outside this very hospital. I never forgot you," Catherine said.

"Did you see who left me?" Emilia asked.

"Oh yes. We talked a long time that night. It wasn't an easy decision to leave, and the person thought about you often over the years," Catherine said.

"Over the years?" Chanel asked.

"You know where my mother is?" Emilia asked softly.

"No. I never met your mother," Catherine said.

"But you said that the two of you talked that night?" Emilia asked.

"I said the person who left you and I talked. The person who left you was not your mother," Catherine replied.

Emilia and Chanel looked at each other not understanding fully what Catherine was saying.

"Who left me then?" Emilia asked.

"Your grandfather. Your mother's father," Catherine answered.

"What? But why? What happened to my mother?" Emilia asked.

"I'm not sure. He never discussed the details. Only to say that this was better for you. That there was too much bad going on in Arbor," Catherine explained.

"Do you know where he is? Can I talk to him?" Emilia asked.

Catherine grew quiet and somber. She bent her head and said, "We had twenty-six wonderful years together. But now he's in there. Your grandfather is my husband."

Emilia looked at the hospital room door nervously.

"Go ahead. I know he would love to see you one last time," Catherine said.

Emilia took a deep breath and walked through the door, leaving Chanel and Catherine behind. She heard the beeping of the heart monitor and saw a frail older black man lying in the hospital bed covered in tubes. Emilia walked up to him slowly and gazed at his sleeping body. She wanted to memorize every inch of his face. This was the first time that she saw someone from her family and she needed the image of him to be engraved in her mind. His skin was a deep dark caramel, and his hair was lightly curled. Emilia could see Elizabeth's cheekbones on him and the shape of her nose. She reached out her hand and gently grabbed hold of his.

The feel of Emilia's hand woke the man, and he gradually opened his eyes and looked up at Emilia. He smiled at Emilia so lovingly that it brought tears to her eyes.

"Lizzie, you came," the man said.

Emilia couldn't speak. He thought she was her mother. How could she tell him she was not? That she was his granddaughter?

"I'm sorry Lizzie. I am so sorry for what I did," he said just before drifting back to sleep.

Emilia quickly let go of his hand. She wondered what he had done to her mother. She wanted to wake him up and make him explain. But the medication wouldn't allow it. Emilia ran out of the room and right up to Catherine. By that time, there was a man who was sitting next to Catherine. But Emilia paid him no attention.

"What did he do to my mother? Why did he keep saying he was sorry?" Emilia asked in hysteria.

"Calm down," the man said as he got up to great Emilia.

"Who are you?" Emilia asked.

"Em. This is Samuel Jones. He's your uncle, I think," Chanel said.

"Hi Emilia," the man said.

"What do you mean my uncle?" Emilia asked.

"Catherine is my mother and Henry, your grandfather, is my father," Samuel explained. "But please call me Sam. My father talked about you. He wanted me to find you someday. I guess you beat me to it."

"Did he talk to you about my mother?" Emilia asked.

"Some," Sam replied.

"Then what is he sorry for?" Emilia asked again.

"That I don't know. All he said was that he had to get out of Arbor and he needed to take you with him. I suspect that whatever happened was so bad that he needed to forget, leave it in his past," Sam explained.

"Do you know?" Emilia asked Catherine.

"No. All he ever said was that he wanted to make sure you were safe and happy." Catherine replied. "I should go back in and be with him. Emilia, your grandfather is a good man. I wish you had a chance to get to know him."

Catherine gave Emilia slight smile and went into Henry's room. Chanel put her arms around Emilia fearing that this may be as far as Emilia would go to find the answers she was searching for.

Sam waited until his mother was in the room and the door was closed behind her. Then he turned to Emilia and Chanel and said, "Something bad definitely happened in Arbor, I just couldn't figure out what it was."

"Why do you say that?" Chanel asked.

"Your mother and I aren't my dad's only children. There's another girl. She's older, from what I can tell. When my dad left, he only took you with him. But he left behind an entire family. Including a wife. They were divorced not too long after my dad came to New York," Sam explained.

"Who is she? Where is she?" Emilia asked feeling like there was still hope left in her search.

"Her name is Odessa Potter. From what I found, she's still in Arbor. I tried to contact her once but didn't really get anywhere," Sam explained. He reached into his pocket and pulled out a piece of paper. "My mother said you are some kind of reporter. I'm merely a Therapist, all of this is foreign to me. So maybe you're just the right person to uncover this mystery," Sam handed Emilia the piece of paper.

"What's this?" Emilia asked.

"It's my father's last known address in Arbor. He never knew I found it," Sam Answered. "I became a therapist to try and fix whatever it was that was eating away at my dad, but I never could reach him."

Emilia stared for a long time at the piece of paper. She felt that this was the clue she was looking for. She just knew that this could lead her to her mother and finally, she could get some answers.

9

Emilia and Chanel arrived at Emilia's apartment trying to figure out what to do next. Emilia kept pacing in deep thought. Her whole world was changing, and things no longer seemed clear to her. So many thoughts were racing through her head, and she couldn't make sense of it all.

Chanel sat there watching as her sister was dealing with the anguish of not knowing who she was and where she came from. A part of her regretted encouraging Emilia to open the folder. She could almost see the heavy load Emilia was now carrying. She couldn't bear seeing her in such a state. Whatever this mystery was could destroy Emilia and Chanel didn't want that to happen.

"What are you thinking?" Chanel asked.

"I'm not really sure," Emilia responded still pacing.

Emilia knew that she had to do something. She needed to figure out what happened to Elizabeth and what Henry was sorry for. Yet the reality of knowing scared her. But not knowing didn't seem to be an option. Emilia took off into her bedroom, and Chanel followed.

"What are you doing?" Chanel asked while watching Emilia standing in her closet.

"I'm going," Emilia said as she reached for an empty suitcase.

"Going where?" Chanel asked.

"I'm going to Arbor," Emilia said as she began to put clothes into the suitcase.

"By yourself?" Chanel asked again sounding concern.

"Yeah. Why not?" Emilia replied.

"Em, you don't know what's waiting for you. There's probably a good reason why Henry never went back or why he took you from there," Chanel told her. "Besides, the fake Elizabeth's story of a biker gang… that just sounds really dangerous."

"It could be dangerous or the problem could be Henry," Emilia said.

"What are you talking about?" Chanel asked.

Emilia stopped packing. She stood face to face with Chanel, and a look of fear came across her face. "What if Henry did something to Elizabeth? What if I'm the product of incest?"

"Ok. Now you're sounding crazy," Chanel replied.

"You think so? We both know anything is possible. I have to go Chanel. I have to find out," Emilia said.

"Ok. I get it. Just give me some time, and I'll go and pack," Chanel said turning to leave.

"No Chanel. I have to do this on my own," Emilia said stopping her.

"I'm not letting you go to dig up some deep dark secret on your own," Chanel said.

"I'll be fine. At the first sign of trouble, I promise to give you a call and I know you'll come running," Emilia told her.

"You better believe it," Chanel said.

Chanel gave Emilia a worried look and then a hug, "Just be careful."

"I will," Emilia responded.

Part II

The Search

10

Emilia's flight landed in the largest city with an airport that was closest to Arbor. Emilia rented a car and begun to make the drive to Arbor. The scenery was beautiful. It was the perfect backdrop for a mild fall day. The leaves were a perfect mixture of red, orange, and brown. Trees and forest surrounded the road leading into Arbor. A sense of calm washed over Emilia as she passed the sign that read, 'Welcome to Arbor.'

Emilia was so captivated by the scenery that she didn't watch how fast she was going. Before she could slow down, she heard the sound of a siren behind her. Emilia slowly pulled over to the side of the road and watched through her rearview mirror as a tall, averagely built white man walked towards her. She rolled down her window allowing him to lean in.

"Ma'am, do you realize how fast you were going?" the man said.

"No, I didn't, officer –" Emilia replied.

"It's Sheriff, ma'am," the man said

"Sorry, Sheriff, but I was in a bit of a hurry," Emilia replied.

Emilia couldn't help but stare at the Sheriff. There was something familiar about him, something that made her feel as if she knew him. There wasn't anything particularly special about him, he looked to be in his mid-forties, handsome, and had that down home country look to him.

"Ma'am there ain't too much around these part for you to be speeding to," the Sheriff replied.

"I'm new in town, but something tells me you probably could tell. Anyway, I'm here to find someone and really wanted to catch her before nightfall," Emilia explained.

"Who are you on your way to see?" the Sheriff asked.

Emilia reached into her pocket and pulled out the piece of paper she got from Sam. "Odessa Potter. She's at this address," Emilia said showing the Sheriff the address on the paper.

"Odessa expecting you?" the Sheriff asked.

"No. She doesn't know I'm coming," Emilia answered.

"You kin to Odessa?" the Sheriff asked again.

"Um. Yes, I guess you can say that," Emilia answered.

"Well, if you kin, then you know Odessa don't like unannounced guest. You best to wait till morning and give her a call letting her know you coming," the Sheriff said.

"Oh. Ok. I guess I can do that," Emilia said. "Are there any hotels nearby?"

The Sheriff stood up tall and smiled, "Follow me, ma'am."

Emilia drove closely behind Sheriff Roberts' car as he led her into the center of town. She parked behind him as he stopped in front of what looked to be an old Victorian house but it had a sign that read 'Bed and Breakfast.'

Emilia got out the car and stood next to it. The Sheriff got out of his car and walked up to her.

"Now on a count of you being new to town and all, I'll let that little speeding thing go. Just make sure you take it easy on our streets," the Sheriff said

"Yes sir I will," Emilia said giving the Sheriff a smile.

"Now you go on in there, and they'll take real good care of you," the Sheriff said.

"Thank you Sheriff," Emilia said

"Folks around these parts call me Sheriff Caleb," he told her as he walked back to his car and got in.

Emilia waited for the Sheriff to drive off before getting her things out from the car and heading to the bed and breakfast. Behind the desk was a nice looking black lady who smiled brightly the moment Emilia walked in.

"How may I help you?" the woman asked.

"I would like a room," Emilia replied.

"For how long?" The woman continued to ask.

"Um. I'm not really sure," Emilia replied.

"How about we put you down for the week, and we can take it from there," the woman said.

"Yes, that would be fine," Emilia said.

The woman grabbed a key from behind the desk and handed it to Emilia. "You will be in the first room, upstairs and to your right. Breakfast starts at 8 am sharp, and my name is Cecilia. If you need anything just give me a holler. My room is right down here, and I don't ever go no where," Cecilia explained with a friendly smile.

"Thank you. I will," Emilia said as she picked up her suitcase and headed up the stairs.

When she got in the room, she flung her suitcase on the bed and took out the piece of paper with Odessa's address on it. Her number was on the bottom, and Emilia stared at it a long time before taking out her cell phone and dialing the number. The phone rang a few times before someone picked up. But they didn't say anything. Emilia could hear the person breathing on the other end.

"Hello. Is this Odessa Potter? Hello?" the phone clicked and then all Emilia could hear was the dial tone.

She held the phone in her hand staring at it. She tried calling back but only got a busy signal. Emilia laid her cell phone down on the end table and tossed herself across the bed next to her suitcase. She was exhausted and needed to rest. Something told her she would need all her strength for when she finally met Odessa.

11

Emilia woke up the next morning to the smell of eggs and bacon. She looked at the time on her cell phone, and it read 7:00 am. Emilia tried to call Odessa one more time, but there was a busy tone. Emilia got up and got herself ready for the day.

She went down the stairs and sat at an already prepared dining room table. There were plates and utensils, and a cheerful Cecilia came in from the kitchen carrying a tray filled with food.

"Well good morning!" Cecilia belted out, "how did we sleep last night?"

"Very comfortably. Thank you," Emilia said.

"Well, it ain't no New York city accommodations, but I like it just the same," Cecilia smiled.

"How did you know I was from New York?" Emilia asked.

"Hunny, we don't get too many out of towners here, so word of you done spread," Cecilia chuckled.

"Really? And what is that word?" Emilia asked again.

"Well. That a really pretty lady from New York is here looking for Odessa," Cecilia said looking at her from the corner of her eye.

"You know Odessa?" Emilia asked.

"This is a small town. We all know each other. I actually grew up across the street from Odessa and her family. Of course, that was some time ago. Before my daddy gambled our house away," Cecilia explained, "so you come all the way from New York City for old crazy ass Odessa?"

"Crazy?" Emilia asked.

"Child Odessa been a mess since we were kids and she really ain't been right since –" Cecilia stopped herself mid-sentence and Emilia could tell she wanted to say more.

"Since when?" Emilia asked.

"Don't mind me. I never too much cared for Odessa." Cecilia got up from the table where she was sitting, "Now go on and finish your breakfast. You want something hot to drink?"

"Um. I could really go for a latté," Emilia replied.

"A lota what? I got coffee. Plain black coffee. How do you take it?" Cecilia responded.

"Cream and sugar will be fine," Emilia said.

As Emilia sat there eating her breakfast, she looked around and noticed that she was the only guest at the bed and breakfast.

"Where are your other guest?" Emilia asked.

"You're it hunny. I told you we don't get too many outa towners around these parts," Cecilia replied.

"How do you make money to survive?" Emilia asked again.

Cecilia chuckled, "You don't need much in Arbor."

Before Emilia could form the next word, the front door opened and Sheriff Caleb came walking in.

"Hey, Cecilia it sure smells good in here," Sheriff Caleb said.

He looked at Emilia and gave her a nod as he took off his hat and sat across the table from her. Cecilia came over to him giving him a hug and placing a plate of food in front of him.

"How are you doing this morning ma'am?" Sheriff Caleb said to Emilia.

"I'm doing just fine Sheriff. Thanks for asking," Emilia replied suspiciously.

"So what are your plans for the day? You looking to go sightseeing?" Sheriff Caleb continued to ask.

"Sheriff Caleb, I believe I told you why I was in town. Now I'm wondering if you're following me for some reason," Emilia replied defensively.

"Ma'am this is my breakfast spot. Cecilia makes the best eggs and bacon in all of North Carolina," Sheriff Caleb said with a chuckle. "But yes, I am curious why you're in town, looking for Odessa of all people."

"Sheriff, the reasons I'm in town are my business and mine alone," Emilia said sternly.

"I can appreciate that. So, tell me, what do you do up there in New York?" Sheriff Caleb continued.

Emilia chuckled, "You're just going to keep at it aren't you?"

"Well, I reckon it's a hazard of the job," Sheriff Caleb said. "I just like to know who's coming into my town."

"That's fair, I guess. I'm a reporter. I work for a newspaper in New York," Emilia answered.

"A Reporter! Why would a reporter be looking for Odessa?" Cecilia asked.

Cecilia and Sheriff Caleb looked at one another with concern on their faces. They began to seem bothered by Emilia's presence. Cecilia grabbed hold of Sheriff Caleb's shoulder as they both stared at Emilia.

"Are you doing a story on Odessa?" Sheriff Caleb asked.

"No. I'm... I think it's time for me to go. Thank you for the breakfast Cecilia," Emilia said as she stood up to leave.

"You're welcome," Cecilia replied with a slight smile.

"I see you around Ma'am," Sheriff Caleb said waving his hand.

12

Emilia found herself sitting outside of Odessa's house, too afraid to get out of her car. She looked around the street and it was quiet and lonely. The houses were not miles apart but they weren't on top of each other either. Odessa's house was old and in need of paint. The grass in the front yard was high and had turned from green to brown. Emilia looked up at the house from her car window and saw shingles that were half off. The stairs looked unsafe, and the windows were dark. The house looked like something out of a horror movie. Emilia was glad she hadn't stopped by the night before. Just looking at the house gave her the feeling of being watched.

Emilia closed her eyes and took a deep breath. She got out of the car and walked up to the house. She walked up the steps onto the rotten front porch and knocked on the door. No one answered. Emilia knocked again and again, no one answered. But this time she thought she heard someone move inside. Emilia tried to look into the nearby window. But it was so dusty and moldy that she could barely see.

"Who the hell are you?" Yelled a voice from behind her.

Emilia turned around quickly to see a petite black woman standing behind her. Her clothes were a few sizes too big, and her hair laid wildly across her head. Her face was tight with anger and annoyance, and her voice was stern and mean.

"I'm looking for Odessa Potter," Emilia said as she walked down the steps to meet the woman.

"Who the hell are you?" the woman asked again as she folded her arms in front of her.

"Are you Odessa?" Emilia asked, but the woman didn't respond.

Emilia took one look at her body language and knew she was Odessa. The time had finally come for Emilia to get some answers about who she was but fear begun to set in. What if what Odessa tells her was even worse than what she had imagined? She thought for sure she was prepared for this moment but now, standing face to face with Odessa, she knew she wasn't.

"I came down here from New York," Emilia said hoping that would make an impression on Odessa, but it didn't. "Um. Henry, your father, is dying in the hospital."

Odessa started to chuckle to herself, and then it turned into a full-blown laughter. "So he went and took his self to New York huh? Well, I ain't sorry and I ain't sending no money for no funeral. Now you take yourself back to New York, and you tell ol Henry that."

Odessa turned to storm off, and something nudged at Emilia. Before she could think she blurted out, "My name is Emilia Elizabeth Long, I'm Lizzie's daughter."

Odessa stopped in her tracks and turned around in rage. She walked back over to Emilia as if she wanted to hit her as hard as she could for saying those words. But she stopped and looked at Emilia up and down, "Lizzie is dead. She ain't never had no kids. I don't know what the hell Henry been filling your head up with, but he ain't nothing but a liar. He deserted his family when we needed him the most, and he ain't never looked back. GET THE HELL OFF MY PROPERTY!"

Odessa's angered startled Emilia, but she was not going to leave like that. She was not going to let Odessa scare her off before she got the answers she was looking for.

"Henry hasn't filled my head with anything. He barely knows who he is these days. I was put up for adoption. I just found out that Lizzie was my mother."

"I said Lizzie ain't never had no kids. If I got to tell you again to get off my property, I will remove you myself," Odessa said.

"I love to see you try Odessa. I'm not going anywhere until I find out where I came from and I how I ended up in New York," Emilia moved in closer to Odessa, "so go ahead try to remove me."

Odessa looked at her in contempt and shook her head, "You just like –"

"Like who Odessa? My mother? Lizzie?" Emilia asked.

"You bout the dumbest lil thing. I told you Lizzie ain't had no kids. Get the hell off my property!"

Just then Sheriff Caleb pulled up and walked over to them. He looked over at the two of them, "Everything alright here?"

Emilia and Odessa stared at each other intensely, neither one of them wanted to break the hold.

"I want her off my property Caleb. I want her off now!" Odessa demanded.

"Now hold on Odessa. What's going on?" Sheriff Caleb asked.

"She says –" Odessa stopped mid-sentence looking at Sheriff Caleb nervously, "She says Henry's in the hospital dying in New York."

"Henry? Your daddy Henry? Oh man, I sure am sorry to hear that," Sheriff Caleb looked over at Emilia, "how much longer he got?"

"A few days, if that," Emilia replied as she noticed the sincere concern on Sheriff Caleb's face.

"I am sorry. But who are you to Henry?" Sheriff Caleb asked.

"She ain't nobody Caleb. If you don't get yourself off my property, I'll have him arrest you for trespassing," Odessa said.

"She ain't lying about that ma'am she's done it plenty of times," Sheriff Roberts said to Emilia.

"Fine. I'll leave, for now. But think about what I said Odessa because I'm coming back. I'm not leaving Arbor without getting what I came for." Emilia walked off leaving Sheriff Caleb and Odessa behind. She got into her car and drove off.

Something inside her told her that Odessa knew more. She could tell that Odessa knew who she was. Emilia became even more determined to find out the truth behind her birth.

13

Emilia sat in her car outside of the Bed and Breakfast. Odessa's behavior towards her had caught her off guard. The level of anger in Odessa's eyes almost overwhelmed Emilia. It wasn't that she expected Odessa to welcome her with open arms, she just didn't expect to be yelled at and treated so badly.

Odessa's behavior and Henry's death bed remorse, solidified in Emilia's mind that something happened, something bad. She went back to her original conclusion, that maybe Henry hurt Lizzie, perhaps Odessa too. That would explain Odessa's anger. Emilia wished she knew how to get through to Odessa, get her to open up to her.

Emilia pressed her head against the staring wheel and exhaled loudly from frustration. She was getting ready to get out of the car when her cell phone rang.

"Hey Sam," Emilia answered after seeing Sam's name light up across her cell phone screen.

"Hey. I just wanted to check on you to see how your first full day in Arbor was coming along," Sam replied.

"Not good at all," Emilia responded.

"Why? What happened?" Sam asked.

"I met Odessa," Emilia answered.

"That's good right?" Sam said.

"Oh, you have no idea. Let's just say it's a good thing you're a Therapist because your sister is certifiable," Emilia explained.

Sam let out a loud laugh and said, "I had a feeling she would be a piece of work. Did she give you anything?

"You mean other than yelling at me and ordering me off her property, no. She did offer to have me arrested," Emilia said.

"Ouch!" Sam yelled.

"But Sam, I think she knows exactly who I am," Emilia said.

"Why do you think that?" Sam asked.

"Because when I called my name, there was something about her face. She knows something Sam I can feel it," Emilia explained.

"Then don't give up or let her drive you away. You deserve to know the truth Emilia," Sam said.

"Yeah. Anyway, how's Henry?" Emilia asked.

"Not good. It could be any day now," Sam answered.

"I'm sorry Sam. I told Odessa about Henry, and she didn't seem to care," Emilia said.

"Well, I figured that," Sam responded.

"Hey, Sam."

"Yeah."

"Is it possible that Henry might have done something to them? You know, something, you know?"

"Like I told you before, it's not possible. You didn't get a chance to get to know him Emilia, but he was the kindest and gentlest man ever. He would never do anything like what you're thinking."

"Ok, but something happened, and I'm not leaving her until I find out what."

"I have no doubt."

Emilia hung up the phone with Sam and went into the Bed and Breakfast. She met Cecilia in the kitchen cooking. She walked in and stood behind Cecilia for a moment watching her.

Cecilia wore a long sundress that had an apron over it. She was a beautiful black woman with hair that laid neatly down her shoulders and happiness running through her body. Cecilia was the type of woman Emilia would dream about when she dreamt of how her birth mother would look and act. She saw Cecilia cooking and dancing in the kitchen and herself, as a little girl, right beside her at the kitchen table dancing right along with her. It was the type of vision that she had forbidden herself to have years ago. But now, being in Arbor and searching for her mother, have brought those visions back.

Cecilia turned around startled to see Emilia standing behind her. She began to giggle and shake her head.

"Why are you just standing there? You scared the dickens out of me," Cecilia said.

"I'm sorry I didn't mean to. You just seem like you were having fun cooking. I didn't want to disturb you," Emilia said.

"Well, I guess I was. I love to cook. Come on in here and have a seat. Are you hungry?" Cecilia said.

"I thought Bed and Breakfast mean I only get breakfast?" Emilia asked.

"Well, I won't tell if you don't. Besides, I'm making lunch for Caleb and there's more than enough left," Cecilia explained.

"Sheriff Caleb? Wait, are you two an item?" Emilia asked.

"No. We're old friends," Cecilia answered.

"You look like you may want more." Emilia said.

"Caleb's heart hasn't been free for anything more than just what we are," Cecilia replied. "Anyway, didn't you go see Odessa today? How did that go?"

"Horrible. She tried to have me arrested for trespassing," Emilia answered.

Cecilia started laughing so hard that tears began to run down her face. "That's Odessa. She's a mean lil somebody. Always have been."

"How mean could you be to not even care that your father is dying?" Emilia asked.

"Oh my lord. Henry is dying?" Cecilia asked grabbing her chest.

"Yes. He has cancer," Emilia answered.

"Poor Henry. I'd always wondered what became of him," Cecilia said.

"You said you and your family lived across the street. What do you remember about Henry?" Emilia inquired.

"He was the sweetest man. Like I said, my daddy gambled like it was going out of style. But Henry always stepped in and helped out my mama whenever he could. I have to call her and tell her about Henry."

"Why is Odessa so mad at him then?"

"Odessa is mad at anything that breathes. She was a lot like her mom. Bee Potter was something scary. I swear I think Henry was most afraid of her."

"If Odessa was like her mom, does that mean Lizzie was like Henry?"

"Um…" Cecilia's face became panicked. She got up from where she was sitting and quickly packed some food in a basket. "I should go take Caleb his lunch before it gets cold. Help yourself to anything on the stove."

Cecilia left in a hurry clearly trying to avoid Emilia's question about Lizzie. Emilia was shocked by Cecilia's action since she seemed so forth coming and open. Emilia wondered what scared Cecilia so much at the mention of Lizzie's name.

"What the hell is going on here?" Emilia said out loud to herself.

14

Emilia sat outside of a small café thinking about her next move and watching people as they went by. She wondered if any of them knew about her mother. Were they around when she died? She noticed that everyone who passed her smiled and greeted her as if they knew her. The town of Arbor was so diverse and friendly that it bewildered Emilia why Henry wanted her away from there.

Emilia also wondered about Lizzie and the mystery sounding her. She wondered if Odessa was lying to her. That maybe Lizzie was somewhere in New York alive. Finding the truth was becoming an addiction for Emilia. She meant what she said to Odessa; she was not leaving Arbor until she found out about Lizzie. She needed to find out when Lizzie died and how.

The waitress, a young blond girl, came out to her table. "Hello, ma'am. What can I get for you?"

"No, I'm fine," Emilia replied. "Um, where is the nearest courthouse?"

"There ain't but one courthouse, and it's about three blocks up the road," the waitress replied pointing in a direction beyond Emilia.

"Thank you," Emilia said.

Emilia figured that if Odessa wasn't going to give her any more information on Lizzie, then she had to find it on her own. She knew that if Lizzie was dead, then there had to be a record about it.

She walked over to the courthouse and went up to the desk. The older white lady smiled at her pleasantly.

"How may I help you?" the woman asked.

"Hi. I'm looking for someone's death certificate," Emilia said.

"Oh my. Well, that's an odd request," the woman said smiling.

"It is public record," Emilia replied.

"Of course it is. We just don't get a lot of those request. Well, not from newcomers anyway," the woman responded. "Whose death certificate are you looking for?"

"The name of the person is Elizabeth Potter," Emilia said.

The woman's face immediately turned serious. Her body tensed up, and she looked frightened. Her face turned almost snow white as if a ghost had just appeared in front of her. She stared at Emilia for a long time, "Why are you… what do you want that for?" the woman asked almost in a whisper.

"Is something wrong?" Emilia asked.

The woman shook her head slowly and with trembling hands, she began to type on her computer. Her face stayed locked in fright and every so often she would cautiously glance up at Emilia. The woman printed the death certificate and hesitantly handed it over to Emilia.

"Thank you," Emilia said as she took the copy of the death certificate from the woman.

Their eyes locked, and Emilia could see a bit of sadness in the woman's eyes. It looked as if she was almost on the brink of tears. Emilia walked away but then stopped; she came back over to the woman asking, "Did you know her?"

The woman looked Emilia in the eye and responded, "No, not really. Just seen her around. I mean, everyone knows everyone around her. But she touched a lot of lives," the woman said, again almost in a whisper.

"How did she touch a lot of lives?" Emilia asked.

"She… she was just an incredible person," the woman replied then she bent her head as if to signal that she was done with answering any further questions. Emilia took one more look at the woman and just knew she had more to say. She wanted to push her some more, but the woman looked so disturbed that Emilia found it almost cruel to continue questioning her.

Emilia walked outside and sat on the steps of the courthouse. She took the death certificate and begun to read it. At first, she just skimmed through it. She first read that Elizabeth's father was Henry Potter and her mother was Bee Potter. Emilia continued to read, and she noticed that the time of death was left blank. Then she went over to the date pronounced dead and while that was filled in, it didn't make sense. The date was months before Emilia was born. How could Lizzie have died before giving birth? Emilia looked down further at the cause of death, and it read 'Murder.'

Emilia froze. "Murder?" Emilia said softly to herself. "By who?" The date Lizzie died could be ignored as a possible typo, but murder wasn't something that could be ignored. That couldn't be a typo. Someone killed Lizzie. Emilia looked back at the courthouse door and realized that perhaps this was why the woman acted so strangely. She got up and ran back in. She ran right back up to the desk. By that time, another woman was standing talking to the woman behind the desk.

"Did they find out who killed her?" Emilia asked hysterically.

The woman lightly shook her head but did not respond. She looked as if she was afraid to speak.

"Did they?!" Emilia shouted.

"You should go talk to the Sheriff ma'am," the other woman said.

"Sheriff Caleb? Why?" Emilia asked.

"He may have better answers for you," the other woman said.

Emilia slowly backed away from the desk as she looked at the two women. She noticed as they grabbed hold of each other's hands and gave one another a side eye. Emilia ran out of the courthouse and didn't stop running until she reached the Sheriff's office, which was one block over.

The black female deputy stood up as Emilia ran in. "Are you alright ma'am? May I help you?"

"I need to speak to the Sheriff, it's important," Emilia said.

"Sheriff Caleb is busy right now. Is there something I can help you with?" the deputy asked.

"No, I need to speak with the Sheriff now. Please."

Just then, Sheriff Caleb poked his head out of his office and said, "It's alright. Come on in ma'am."

Emilia walked into Sheriff Caleb's office and sat down on the chair across from his desk. The Sheriff sat at his desk and had concern on his face as he looked at Emilia.

"Everything alright? You didn't go back over to Odessa's did you?" Sheriff Caleb asked.

"No. I went to the courthouse and pulled Elizabeth Potter's death certificate," Emilia said.

The Sheriff's concerned face turned to panic and then sadness. His eyes looked like they were about to tear up, just like the woman in the courthouse. Emilia wondered why the name bothered everyone so much. What was it about Lizzie that causes everyone to have such strong reactions?

"What did you do that for?" the Sheriff asked.

"Because Odessa didn't want to tell me," Emilia replied.

"What is it about Lizzie that you need to know?" the Sheriff asked again.

"For starters, who killed her?" Emilia asked.

Sheriff Caleb got up and walked over to the window. He stared through them as if he was looking at a magical creature in the distance. His mind seemed to wander off, and Emilia knew that he had gone somewhere different.

"Sheriff Caleb," Emilia called out to get his attention again.

"Yes. I'm sorry," Sheriff Caleb said turning to look at her slightly.

"Who killed her?" Emilia repeated.

"No one was found," Sheriff Caleb said as if it pained him.

"So the case was just dropped? Were there any clues or witnesses?" Emilia asked as she sat on the edge of her seat.

Sheriff Caleb shook his head. "I can't tell you that. I was just a kid myself."

"Can I see the police report?" Emilia asked.

Sheriff Caleb turned to look at her. "Those things are all archived somewhere; I can't begin to tell you where they are. Besides, you don't have much right to see those things, and I think you know that."

Emilia looked at Sheriff Caleb and wanted to blurt out that she had all the rights in the world. That she was

Lizzie's daughter. But the words couldn't come out. She stood up and turned to walk away.

"Ma'am, I suggest you get whatever Henry sent you here for and leave. Ain't no need digging up old bones; you may not like what you find," Sheriff Caleb said.

Emilia walked out without saying a word. She felt defeated. It was as if Lizzie was this town's dark secret and everyone wanted to keep her that way.

15

One thing had become clear, Emilia had to dig into what happened to Lizzie the night she disappeared. She just didn't know how. The entire town had seemed to have closed that chapter and was refusing to reopen it. Emilia had to find another way.

She was sitting in her car considering all her options when the female deputy Sheriff came outside. Emilia looked around to make sure Sheriff Caleb was not somewhere looking, then she got out of her car and slowly approached the female deputy Sheriff.

"Hi," Emilia said to her.

"Hello, ma'am. Is there something I can help you with?" the female Sheriff said.

"No. I just wanted to apologize for my behavior a few minutes ago. I'm really sorry. It's just that I'm a reporter and I'm writing a story on Sheriff Caleb and his work in this town. I just felt like he didn't give me the full information on something and it really bothered me," Emilia explained. She knew she was lying, but she had to see what the Deputy Sheriff knew.

"It's not a problem ma'am. Are you really doing a story on the Sheriff?" the Deputy asked.

"Absolutely. I mean this town is probably one of the last few peaceful towns left. There aren't any prisoners in your cells. You guys probably don't even keep case records in the office because there probably aren't any cases," Emilia said with a chuckle.

"Well, you're right about that ma'am. Most of our stuff is electronic now anyway," the Deputy said.

"Even your old case files. I know being from New York, there are just boxes and boxes of old case files all over the place," Emilia responded.

"Well, we don't have many old cases. What we do have we keep in the basement of the library," the Deputy replied.

"Really. That's interesting," Emilia said. She knew Sheriff Caleb was lying when he said he didn't know where the archived records were. Now, all Emilia had to do was get to those files.

"I reckon it is," the Deputy said. "I got to get going but good luck on your story. The Sheriff deserves some recognition."

"Of course and again, I'm really sorry for earlier," Emilia said.

She quickly got into her car and found her way to the library. There weren't a lot of people inside, just a few teens and one or two older people.

Emilia looked over at the librarian behind the desk and then acted like she was searching for a book. She walked down the aisles for a while before going up to the librarian to ask where the bathroom was.

The librarian told her that it was down the hall. Emilia walked in that direction but had no intention of using the bathroom. She had to find the door leading to the basement. Emilia walked to the end of the hall towards the red sign that said exit. It hung over a large gray door. Emilia looked around her for any other doors. But there were none.

She then looked back over at the door wondering whether there was an alarm on it. No warning signs or wires were indicating an alarm.

Emilia gently pushed the door opened and closed her eyes tightly anticipating an alarm to go off. It didn't. She walked through the door which led to a stairwell. There were stairs that led up and stairs that lead down. The library was on the main floor, so it wasn't hard for Emilia to conclude that the stairs leading down would take her to the basement.

The basement was dark and drafty. She only saw one door. Emilia walked up to the door and again examined it before he tried to open it. She turned the door knob slowly, and the door opened. Emilia looked around in shock. She didn't think it would be that easy.

Emilia walked into a small room, the size of a large walk-in closet. The room was dark. Emilia noticed a rope hanging from the ceiling. She looked up and saw one lightbulb attached to that rope. Emilia pulled the rope and turned on a low beam light.

She was able to see the shelves that were in the room. It was barely empty except for a few boxes that had labels on them. Emilia looked on all the boxes to see if they had names. They did, just not the name Elizabeth Potter.

One box did have the same date that Lizzie disappeared. But the name on it said, Randel Jamison. Emilia took that box down and opened it. There were bloodied clothes wrapped in plastic and a wallet. Emilia opened the wallet to find a driver's license for Randel Jamison. His picture and his date of birth put him at just about the same age as Lizzie, maybe a year or two older.

Emilia looked in the box again, but that was it. She heard a noise and quickly put the box back where she found it. She pulled the rope above her head again to turn the light off. She slowly poked her head out of the door but didn't see anyone. She made her way back up the stairs that led to the library and out of the door to her car.

All the way back to the bed and breakfast, Emilia wondered who Randel Jamison was and why the date on a box with his name matched the same date Lizzie went missing.

16

Emilia sat on her bed with every piece of paper she had on Lizzie. Those pieces of paper were all that she had to put together the puzzle of what happened to Lizzie. She stared at the death certificate and then at the newspaper clippings. Yet nothing was making sense. She read the newspaper articles over and over again, especially the one about Lizzie being missing. It said that the whole community searched for her for days. Yet there was nothing that discussed how she ended up missing and the name Randel Jamison didn't appear in any of them.

Then all of a sudden something peculiar caught Emilia's eyes. The date on the newspaper article was only a few days before Lizzie was declared dead. Emilia sat up straight in her bed holding the newspaper article in one hand and the death certificate in the other. She just kept looking back and forth at them with a puzzled look on her face.

The dates were wrong she thought to herself. But why? Why does it have Lizzie going missing and dying months before Emilia was born? When Emilia first saw the date, Lizzie went missing, she thought that at some point, somehow, Lizzie came home. She thought all she had to figure out was what happened to Lizzie from the time she had her baby until her death. But Emilia really needed to figure out how someone could give birth months after their death.

Emilia wondered if her birth certificate was wrong. Maybe Lizzie wasn't her mother. But then who was her mother and how did she end up with Henry in New York? What about that note that was left with her. Who wrote it? Was it Lizzie, Henry, or her real mother?

Emilia had more questions than answers and her head was spinning. She laid down both pieces of paper in frustration and reached for her phone. There was an answer after a few rings. "Hello."

"Hey Chanel," Emilia responded.

"Are you ok?" Chanel asked.

"Nope," Emilia replied.

"What happened?" Chanel continued to ask.

"It's the weirdest thing Chanel. Everything I find on Lizzie says she died months before I was born," Emilia explained.

"How is that possible?" Chanel asked.

"I don't know," Emilia answered.

"Well, did you find this Odessa person?"

"Yeah, but she was no help. She was just so angry and mean," Emilia explained.

"You've come this far Em. Someone in that town has to know what happened to her," Chanel said.

"That's just it. I know they do. But every time I even mention her name, everyone tensed up. I don't know what they're hiding. Even the Sheriff warned me not to dig up bones or something crazy like that," Emilia replied.

"Em, ma found those newspaper articles on Lizzie, maybe there's more out there," Chanel said.

"None that I've found," Emilia replied somberly. "But there is something."

"What?" Chanel asked.

I sort of snuck into the Sheriff's archived records and there was a box about a boy who died the same date Lizzie went missing," Emilia explained.

"That can't be a coincidence," Chanel said. "What's his name?"

"Randel Jamison," Emilia said.

Emilia could hear Chanel typing away again on her keyboard. She waited anxiously to see what Chanel would find out.

"The only article on him is that he was murdered in the woods there in Arbor. There's not much else," Chanel said.

"Oh," Emilia replied sounding disappointed.

"Wait, let me check something else," Chanel said.

"What?" Emilia asked.

"The FBI database," Chanel replied.

"Are you crazy?" Emilia asked in a panic. "You know you could get in serious trouble for that, right? And what would a small town's murder be doing in the FBI database anyway?"

"So, which question do you want me to answer first?" Chanel asked sarcastically. "How about you already know I'm a bit crazy, yes I know I could get in trouble which is why I keep bill money, and it's in there because apparently it was classified as a hate crime."

"Wait, what? Seriously?" Emilia asked.

"Yeah. According to this, he appeared to have been beaten and his skull smashed in," Chanel said.

"Oh my God. Anything about Lizzie?"

"Yeah. According to witnesses, she was in the woods that night too. She could not be found. She was declared dead after weeks of searching for her."

"So why did they think it was a hate crime?"

"The then Sheriff believed that a group of white boys who were known to be racist were the ones who did it. Guess they couldn't prove it."

"Could those boys have been bikers?" Emilia asked

"It doesn't say," Chanel answered. "Who do you think Randel was to Lizzie?"

"Maybe… maybe he was my father." Emilia said almost in whisper.

"Ok. Wait Em, don't get ahead of yourself. So she's in the woods with this boy, how did she end up missing?" Chanel replied.

"I don't know." Emilia answered.

"Ok Em, I'm a little weirded out. Small towns don't like their secrets coming out plus those guys could still be in Arbor. Em, I think you have enough information, come home."

"No Chanel I don't have enough information. If he was my father, then I need to know what happened to him too. Why were he and Lizzie in the woods that night? I have to know Chanel."

"Em…."

"Chanel, I promise I'll be fine. The moment I think it's getting too dangerous, I'll leave."

"I don't know about this Em. Maybe I should come."

"No Chanel. Let me do this."

"Promise me you'll be safe Em."

"I promise."

"Ok. I'll send you everything I found. Please be careful."

"Thanks Chanel. I will."

Emilia hung up the phone from Chanel and went about finding anything she could on Randel. She managed to find his sister who was still living in Arbor. Emilia wrote down the sister's address. She hoped that she was finally getting closer to the truth.

17

The next morning, Emilia woke up ready to gather more pieces to the puzzle. She went downstairs and was greeted by more of Cecilia's cooking. When Emilia walked into the dining room, Cecilia smiled at her awkwardly. She was not her usual cheerful self. Emilia sat down keeping one eye on Cecilia. Cecilia came over and poured her a cup of coffee then walked away without making eye contact.

When Cecilia came back into the dining room, she placed a plate in front of Emilia, still not making eye contact. Emilia could sense that something was going on with Cecilia and figured the news of the nature of her visit had reached Cecilia.

"So I guess you know why I'm here?" Emilia asked.

"No, not really. All I know is you bringing up things that should be left alone," Cecilia said with her back to Emilia.

"Things like what, Lizzie?" Emilia asked again.

Cecilia was holding a serving tray in her hand that dropped at the mention of Lizzie's name. Her back was still turned to Emilia, but Emilia could sense genuine pain coming from Cecilia.

"What is it, Cecilia? Why do everyone react the way they do when I say Lizzie's name?"

Cecilia finally turned to face Emilia with tear filled eyes, "Some pains are better left unspoken." Cecilia walked away and went into her room closing the door behind her.

Emilia couldn't eat, she got in her car and began to drive. The information that Chanel emailed to her said that Randel had a sister by the name of Olive Johnson. Chanel was also able to find an address that led her just outside of town to a beautiful tree-lined street with gorgeous family friendly homes.

Emilia stopped and parked her car just outside a beige two story house with a large front porch. When Emilia was younger, she used to dream about growing up in a place like this. She used to wonder if her real family lived like this. Emilia's eyes glanced up and down the peaceful street. She looked out of her car window at the house with its perfectly manicured lawn.

Emilia worked up the nerves to get out of her car and walk up to the door. She rang the doorbell and immediately became nervous. She turned around, about to walk away, when the door opened, and a woman stood in the door way. Emilia stared at the woman to see if she saw some resemblance. If Randel was her father, then maybe she would look like his sister. But the woman's complexion was darker, her face was rounder, and her height was shorter.

"May I help you?" the woman asked.

"Hi. I'm Emilia Long." Emilia said pulling out her card and giving it to the woman.

"A Reporter? Is everything ok?" the woman said.

"Yes, everything is fine. I'm looking for Olive Johnson," Emilia said.

"Well, I'm Olive Johnson. But what would a Reporter want with me?" Olive answered.

"Mrs. Johnson this is going to sound really weird but I'm from New York, and I came down to look into what happened to your brother Randel and Lizzie." Emilia stood back and waited for Olive to have the same reaction as everyone else. For that look of panic and fright to come across her face.

But it didn't. Olive looked at Emilia for a long time and then said, "Are you serious?"

"Yes, I am," Emilia replied.

"And you think you can find out?" Olive asked again.

"Yes, I do," Emilia answered.

"Then come in." Olive opened her screen door wider to let Emilia in.

Emilia walked into Olive's house, and she could tell that children lived there. There were toys scattered neatly around. There were family portraits along the wall that showed a happy family.

"You have a beautiful family," Emilia commented.

"Thank you," Olive replied and led Emilia to the sitting room. "Would you like anything to drink?"

"No, I'm fine," Emilia replied. "Can you tell me what you remembered from that night?"

"Well, we're just going to jump right in it huh," Olive said with a smile. "I was twelve. Randel was my awesome big brother. I used to sneak around his room to eaves drop on his conversations. But there weren't much conversations going on. Randel was all about the books. He never went out at night, he just studied. But that night, he got a call and then ran out from his room almost running me over. He said that he had to go and do something and to tell mom and dad that he'll be back. He kissed me on the forehead before he left and told me he loved me." Olive's eye swelled with tears as she remembered that moment.

Emilia saw how painful it was for Olive, but she needed more, "Where did he say he was going?"

"He didn't." Olive answered

"Do you know who was on the phone?" Emilia asked.

"No." Olive replied.

"Could it have been Lizzie?" Emilia asked again.

"I doubt it." Olive answered with a chuckle. "Lizzie never called my brother although he would have been on the moon if she did."

"So, they weren't dating?"

"Oh heavens no. My brother was head over heels for Lizzie, but I don't think she shared the same feelings for him."

"Why didn't you think so?"

"Well, one day, months before he died. He took me to this dinner. A real popular spot for teens. Lizzie and her friends were there. My brother spent most of the time staring at her. She barely looked at him once. She even passed by to go to the counter and he tried to say hi, but she was talking to some other guy and didn't even acknowledge my brother."

"Then why were they both in the woods?"

"That's a good question. I told them he got a call before he left but no one paid me any attention. I guess they figured I was just a kid, what did I know?"

Emilia listened to Olive, and it was obvious that Randel wasn't her father. But there was still a question of how he ended up in the woods with Lizzie and what happened to Lizzie.

"Mrs. Johnson, did Lizzie ever show up after that night?"

"Nope. About a week or two after, they declared her dead."

"Without a body?"

"There was a lot of theories about what happened in that woods that night."

"What was the story you heard?"

"That Randel interrupted someone hurting Lizzie and they killed him and her. At first, everyone thought that maybe the person buried Lizzie. But they dugged up every inch of those woods; my father helped, and they found nothing. So, everyone came to the conclusion that the person must have thrown her body in the river below the hill. The Sheriff said her body could be anywhere. But they still put on scuba suits and dived right in. But nothing."

"Did they ever find out who did it?"

"No. But Arbor still went a little crazy."

"Why?"

"Some people passing said they heard a fighting and carrying on, then they saw some kids, teenagers, running from the woods. They were all white. They said they all jumped on bikes and had those crazy jackets with skulls and graffiti on them. The thought that Lizzie and my brother, two black teens, were killed by some racist group of white kids. Well, it almost destroyed Arbor. It took a long time for Arbor to come back. People moved. Whites stayed with whites; blacks stayed with blacks. The soul of Arbor left that night."

"But everyone seemed to get along so well now."

"Because they have put that night away and locked it up, never to be discussed again."

"What about you? What do you think happened?"

"I don't have a clue. Maybe it was some hateful act. Maybe it was a prank gone wrong. Maybe there was a masked man in the woods killing teenagers. Maybe it was a ghost. Who knows, all I know is my brother is gone, and an entire town acts as if he never existed."

"This may sound like a crazy question, but were there any sightings of Lizzie after that night?"

"Not that I heard of, and trust me, that would have been news. But of course, my family moved from Arbor not too long after. I attempted to go back, but this is the furthest I've gotten."

Olive smiled with her eyes as she turned to look at a picture on the wall. The picture was of Randel. He looked happy. Emilia knew that she hadn't gotten a lot of her questions answered, but for the first time, she actually felt like she was getting somewhere. Now she had to figure out what her next move would be. There had to be someone else in that town that knew more about Lizzie and was willing to talk to her. She just had to find that person.

18

Emilia got back to the bed and breakfast with her head still spinning from what Olive had told her. Her hopes of not only finding out what happened to her mother but also finding her father had been dashed. Randel was not her father. He was a guy who was in love with Lizzie. Emilia still wondered what Lizzie was doing in the woods that night with Randel if she didn't return his feelings.

Emilia sat on the white rocking chair on the porch of the bed and breakfast. She looked out onto the sun laced streets and wondered what it was like when Lizzie walked them. Did people greet her with warmth or was she hated and treated poorly? Did she smile joyfully or was there sadness in her eyes?

The cool breeze swept across Emilia's face softly and for a moment she thought she saw Lizzie walking down the street. She wanted to reach out to her, to grab her and hug her tightly without letting go.

The image of Lizzie was quickly interrupted by the sound of her phone ringing. Emilia reached into her pocket and pulled out her phone. She answered it without looking to see who was calling.

"How's my private detective doing?" the male voice on the other end of the phone asked.

Emilia recognized the voice immediately. It was Sam. "I'm hanging in there I guess," Emilia replied.

"Did you get to talk with Odessa again?" Sam continued to ask.

"No, not yet," Emilia replied.

"Are you alright?" Sam asked.

"Yeah. There's just so many unanswered questions," Emilia answered.

"Well, if anybody could get those questions answered, you can," Sam said.

"Yup I hope so. So how's Henry?"

"Um… I'm sorry Emilia, but he passed late last night."

"Oh no." Emilia rested her head on her hand, and a wave of sadness and regret began to consume her heavily.

She wanted to get to know Henry. To know where she came from. No matter how she came into this world, Henry cared enough to make sure she was safe. He brought her to a hospital and made sure she was taking care of. She wanted to thank Henry for that. A tear fell down her face and her heart began to break.

"I'm sorry Emilia," Sam said.

"No. I barely got a chance to know him. How are you and your mom doing?" Emilia responded.

"Well, I'm being strong. I'm worried about my mother though. She loved him a lot."

"Um. I'm coming home."

"No, don't do that. My dad would have wanted you to know, and you have to stay until you find out what that is."

"No one wants to talk to me Sam. They all act as if Lizzie was some sort of horror story."

"What do you mean?"

"It's nothing. You're right, Henry would have wanted me to stay, I have to find out what happened to Lizzie."

"Are you sure you're alright Emilia?"

"Yes of course. Keep me posted on the funeral arrangements. And give your mother my best."

"I will. Emilia, if you need me I'm there."

"Thanks, Sam."

Emilia hung up the phone from Sam and was numb. Her hands covered her face, and the world seemed to disappear.

"Are you alright?" Cecilia had gotten home from grocery shopping and was now standing on the steps of the front porch looking at Emilia with concern in her eyes.

Emilia lifted her eyes and tried to hide her distress. But her heart was too heavy.

"Henry passed last night," Emilia said.

"Oh no. I'm so sorry," Cecilia replied, "is there anything I can do?"

Emilia chuckled to herself, "Can you tell me what the hell happened to Lizzie. The sooner I find out the sooner I can go home."

Cecilia walked up the stairs nervously. She walked passed Emilia while avoiding eye contact and went into the house with the bags of groceries. Seconds later, she came back out without the groceries and sat down next to Emilia.

Cecilia looked far out into the distance and said, "I don't know what happened that night. But I can tell you she was an amazing person."

"You knew her?" Emilia asked.

"She was my best friend," Cecilia answered.

Emilia turned to look at Cecilia. "She was?

"Yes, ma'am. We had been friends since we were kids. That girl was something else." Cecilia said and then looked at Emilia with a smile on her face. "You know you remind me a lot of her. You definitely got her spirit."

Emilia smiled. This was the first time someone had compared her to Lizzie. "What was she like?"

"Oh. She was the apple of everybody's eye. Everyone loved Lizzie. She was the captain of the cheerleading team but not in a snobby type of way. No, not Lizzie. She was special. She cared about people and had a huge heart."

"Then who would want to hurt her?"

"That I don't know."

"Why was she in the woods that night?"

"Because that was the hangout spot."

"Hang out spot?"

"Yeah. See, as a teenager, there wasn't much we could do for fun in Arbor, there still ain't. So, we all use to gather in the woods and drink, play music, and just party."

"Randel too?"

"No. Randel was a bit of a loner. He was always focused on his books. He really wasn't part of, you know, the crowd."

"You mean the popular crowd?"

"I guess you can say that," Cecilia chuckled.

"Was Randel resentful of that?"

"I never really took the time to find out."

"His sister said that he was in love with Lizzie."

"That was obvious. A lot of guys were in love with Lizzie."

"She just didn't care for him?"

"I don't know. She never talked about him. But Lizzie couldn't even return Randel's feelings even if she wanted to."

"Why not?"

"While Randel was desperately in love with Lizzie, Odessa was desperately in love with Randel."

"What?"

"Oh yes. They'd been friends since elementary school or something like that, but he never saw her as anything more than a friend, at least I don't think so."

"How was Odessa and Lizzie's relationship?"

"She treated Lizzie about the same way she treated you when you went by her house the other day," Cecilia laughed out loud, "the way she was yelling and fussing about you getting off her property. That's Odessa for you. You just had to deal with that for one day. Lizzie had to deal with it for sixteen years."

Emilia thought for a moment. She wondered if the reason Henry had taken her to New York was not to protect her from the town of Arbor, but to protect her from Odessa. Emilia stood up and began to walk towards the steps.

"Where are you going?" Cecilia asked.

"I have to go tell miss personality that her father died," Emilia responded.

"Well good luck with that," Cecilia replied with a smirk.

19

Odessa was working in her backyard when Emilia showed up to the house. Emilia walked over to the back of the house when she heard the sound of shoveling. Emilia stood quietly behind Odessa for a moment just watching her. Odessa was s petite woman but seemed powerful in stature. Her clothes always looked too big, and her hair was always curly and wild.

Anger and resentment poured out of her without her having to say a word. Her surrounding screamed loneliness, yet Emilia thought Odessa liked it that way.

"You just gonna stand there?" Odessa said to Emilia with her back still turned.

"How did you know I was here?" Emilia asked.

Odessa stood up and looked Emilia in the eye. "You got the stench of city on you."

"That's lovely Odessa," Emilia replied sarcastically.

"What the hell you want?" Odessa asked.

"Henry died last night," Emilia announced watching the unchanged expression on Odessa's face.

"What do you want me to do about it?" Odessa asked

"He was your father Odessa; I just thought you would like to know," Emilia replied.

"Well, now I know. Now leave," Odessa said.

"Why are you always in such a hurry to get rid of me? Is it because you're scared I'll find out the truth?" Emilia asked.

"Ain't no truth to find little girl," Odessa responded.

"Yes there is, and I think I've figured parts of it out," Emilia said.

"Oh have you now?" Odessa said.

"Yes, I have," Emilia leaned in closer to Odessa, "Lizzie was in the woods that night maybe to hang out with her friends, it was the hangout spot. Randel somehow ended up in the woods. I'm pretty sure someone called him and sent him there. Somehow Randel ended up dead, and Lizzie saw it happen. Maybe she took off scared and was hiding or maybe someone was protecting her from what she saw or from whoever did it. But all I know is Lizzie's alive, at least long enough to give birth to me. My only question for you Odessa is, where's Lizzie?"

Odessa began to laugh and started walking away from Emilia.

"Laugh all you want Odessa but you know I'm right," Emilia said walking behind her.

Odessa stopped walking and turned to look at Emilia, "You don't know nothing little girl. All you got is gossip."

"I got me Odessa. The fact that I'm standing here proves that Lizzie didn't die that night," Emilia said.

"Don't nothing prove nothing," Odessa replied in anger.

"What are you so afraid of? Your mother died, Henry's dead, all that's left is us Odessa. So what do you think I'm going to do when I find Lizzie? What trouble do you think I'm going to cause? Why are you so afraid of me

Odessa?" Emilia fired off questions at Odessa hoping that she would at least answer one of them.

"I ain't afraid of you little girl. I just want you off my property." Odessa was clearly un-phased by Emilia's questions.

Odessa turned around again and walked into the house slamming the door behind her. Emilia looked around and noticed that from the backyard of Odessa's house was a clear entrance into the woods. It was getting dark, and Emilia thought it best to head back to the bed and breakfast since she had walked to Odessa's house. But something kept pulling at her to go.

She looked up at Odessa's house to see if Odessa was in the window looking at her. When she didn't see Odessa there, she began to walk into the woods.

The trees were so tall that it was almost as if they were touching the sky. The trail was dirty, long, and damp. But once Emilia reached the clearing, she could see why teenagers used to like to hang out there. It was secluded yet mesmerizing. Emilia could hear the raging water down below the embankment. She slowly walked over to the edge and looked over. She then turned around and observed the woods behind her. She wondered where Randel's body was found. She could see why folks felt that Lizzie's body might be somewhere in these woods, there was a lot of square miles, and someone could easily get lost in it.

Emilia turned back to the river below and stared down at it. She so wished that the trees had a voice and they could tell her what happened in those woods all those years ago.

"Lizzie!" A male voice called out to Emilia in a whisper, "My God Lizzie is that you?"

Emilia quickly turned around to see the shocked expression on Sheriff Caleb's face.

"What?" Emilia asked while walking out of the shadows and towards Sheriff Caleb.

"Oh, Ms. Long. What are you doing in the dark?" Sheriff Caleb said as he tried to compose himself.

"You called me Lizzie," Emilia said.

Sheriff Caleb had said that he and Lizzie went to high school together. But in that moment, Emilia realized that Sheriff Caleb might have known Lizzie more than he was letting on.

"Why did you call me Lizzie?" Emilia asked.

"It doesn't matter. Come on let's get you out of these woods."

Sheriff Caleb ushered her out of the woods while looking at her peculiarly. Something was telling Emilia that Sheriff Roberts knew something and she had to find out what that something was.

20

The next morning, Emilia waited for Sheriff Caleb to come to Cecilia's bed and breakfast so that she could ask him how well he knew Lizzie. But Sheriff Caleb never showed up.

Emilia left Cecilia's and went for a walk. She spotted Sheriff Caleb sitting inside of the small café. Emilia went in and sat at the table across from him. He was reading a newspaper but put it down the moment Emilia sat down.

"Ms. Long. How are you this morning?" Sheriff Caleb asked.

"Still looking for answers Sheriff," Emilia replied.

Sheriff Caleb chuckled to himself and placed his newspaper down on the table. He stared for a long time at Emilia and smiled.

"About what Ms. Long?" Sheriff Caleb asked.

"About what happened last night," Emilia replied.

"Well, last night I reckon I had a little too much to drink." Sheriff Caleb replied.

"I don't think so. I think you thought you saw Lizzie and it sounded like you were happy about it," Emilia said.

Sheriff Caleb's face turned serious. He motioned to the waitress for the check. After he had paid, he stood up and told Emilia to go for a walk with him. Emilia followed Sheriff Caleb out of the café, and they walked down the street. They were quiet at first until they got to a small park that sat in the middle of the town. Sheriff Caleb sat on the green bench, and Emilia sat next to him.

Emilia could see a distant look in Sheriff Caleb's eyes, and she wondered where he went. She turned her body to face him, and that immediately got his attention.

"That night isn't something folks around here forgot about," Sheriff Caleb said.

"I heard it started some sort of race war," Emilia said.

"I guess you could say that," Sheriff Caleb responded.

"Cecilia said that the woods were where the popular kids hung out," Emilia said with a slight smile.

"That's right," Sheriff Caleb nodded.

"So, were you there that night?" Emilia asked.

"You're assuming I was popular," Sheriff Caleb said with a smile.

"I am. So what happened?" Emilia asked again.

"We just won the regional football championship," Sheriff Caleb answered.

"You were on the football team?" Emilia asked.

"I was the captain," he replied.

"And you guys went to celebrate?" Emilia continued to ask.

"That's right," he answered.

"Lizzie was there," Emilia said.

"She was."

"What happened?"

"Some boys, bikers of some sort, came and was starting some mess. The boys were from the two towns over, and all white. They got into it with some of the players on our team."

"The black players."

"Yes."

"Then what happened?"

Sheriff Caleb scratched his face like he was nervous. He bent his head as if he was ashamed, "Some of us, including me, left."

"Why?"

"It wasn't our fight."

"But why would you-"

"Listen, we didn't think anything was going to happen. Them boys were just drunk and looking for a fight."

"But something did happen Sheriff."

Sheriff Caleb sat back and looked up to the sky. He had guilt all over his face, and Emilia felt sorry for him.

"What happened to everyone who was involved?" Emilia asked.

"Most of the black players' parents took off and moved them out of town. They were all my friends. Some were the best friends I ever had."

"What about those boys, did anyone investigate them for what happened to Randel and Lizzie?"

"Yup. One of them, who folks felt was the ringleader, was investigated. He was in town visiting his mother."

"What did they come up with?"

"Not enough evidence to link him to Randel and Lizzie's death."

"Where is he now?"

"Last I heard he was locked up on drug charges."

"What about his mother? Is she still in Arbor?"

"She sure is. She went through a lot during those days."

"Who is she? Where is she?"

"I believe you already met her."

"I have?"

"Yup. She's the clerk over at the courthouse."

Emilia's mind immediately ran to the lady at the courthouse. She could see the fright in her face at merely hearing Lizzie's name. Now it all made sense. Her son was probably one of the ones who killed Randel. Maybe he did something to Lizzie too, something so horrifying that it made her run and hide, escaping this town like so many others had after that night.

Emilia stood up and quickly started to make her way over to the courthouse. Sheriff Caleb was yelling at her, but she couldn't hear him. She had to get to the courthouse and find out what the woman knew.

When Emilia got to the courthouse, it was practically empty. She walked right up to the clerk's desk and came face to face with the woman standing behind it.

It was the same woman. Her face was slightly wrinkled and harden. She barely smiled and looked as if she was preparing herself for a battle.

"Why didn't you tell about your son?" Emilia asked without even saying hello.

"You didn't ask," the woman replied.

"I'm asking now. Did your son kill Randel?"

"My son ain't do no such thing. Ever since that night, he been saying that he ain't hurt nobody. Folks around here don't like that you been putting your nose where it doesn't belong."

"Where does it belong Mrs. -" Emilia looked down and saw the woman's name on the name tag sitting on the desk. "Hatcher."

"This town let that tragic night go and you ain't nothing but the devil trying to come here and bring it back up again," she said.

"Your son might have killed someone because of the color of their skin. How can that be forgotten." Emilia watched as Mrs. Hatcher's face turned mournful. "What did he tell you about that night?"

"He ain't tell me nothing. Just that he was out trying to have a little fun with his friends. My son ain't been right since that night. He been in and out of jail, messing with that drug. He ain't kill nobody. Please, just leave it alone." Mrs. Hatcher began to cry and she turned and walked away.

Emilia walked out of the courthouse and sat on the steps convinced she had found another piece of the puzzle.

Emilia went back to the park, but Sheriff Caleb was gone. She immediately ran to the Sheriff's office and didn't stop until she was standing at Sheriff Caleb's desk. She was panting and out of breath. This was the first big clue that she had to finding out what happened to Lizzie. Emilia felt like she was getting close.

"Can you get me in to see him?" Emilia asked hysterically.

"To see who?" Sheriff Caleb asked as he sat back in his chair.

"The guy who was the suspect. You said he was in jail somewhere so I can't just walk in but you can get me in," Emilia explained.

Sheriff Caleb stood up and walked around his desk. He looked Emilia in the eye and said, "You got to let this go."

"I can't," Emilia replied.

"Why not? It doesn't matter what happened that night. Even if you and Odessa are fighting over your father's property."

"My father? What did Odessa tell you about me?"

"Nothing much. She just said that Henry had gone on to New York and started a new family. I'm assuming that family included you."

Emilia stood up straight and stared at Sheriff Caleb for a long time. She knew she had to tell him the truth about who she was no matter how crazy it may sound to him. Emilia took a deep breath and said, "Henry isn't my father. He's my grandfather."

Sheriff Caleb looked at her confused, "How is that possible?"

"Lizzie was my birth mother."

Sheriff Caleb stood up shaking his head furiously. He walked over to the window in disbelief. "That's not possible. Lizzie didn't have any kids before she died."

"Apparently I was born after she died."

Sheriff Caleb turned around instantly, "What?!"

"They lied, the whole family lied. Lizzie didn't die in the woods that night."

"Lizzie died Ms. Long. I don't know what Henry told you, but Lizzie is gone."

"Henry didn't tell me much of anything. He brought me to New York after I was born and left me at a hospital. I was adopted."

Sheriff Caleb's eyes danced around, not able to land in one place. "Get out of my office please," he said to her in a low tone.

Sheriff Roberts began to usher Emilia out of his office. She tried to plea to him, but he didn't want to hear it. He escorted her out of his office and closed the door behind her. Emilia stood outside not knowing what to do next.

21

It was mid-afternoon the next day before Emilia was finally able to get someone to help her. A source of hers who was a Federal Prosecutor had connections with local jails in the area. After Emilia explained to her what was going on, she was more than happy to help. She found out that a Brady Hatcher was an inmate at a jail 50 miles from Arbor. She got Emilia special clearance to see him.

Emilia took the drive to see Brady. All the way there she wondered what he would tell her. Would he be willing to come clean or give her some hint as to what happened to Lizzie after Randel was killed? There was a nervous knot in the pit of Emilia's stomach. She wondered if these guys had done something to Lizzie, something horrible. Being in the news business, she had run into situations where rape victims just up and disappear never to be heard from again. They rather leave than face the pain of what happened to them. She wondered if that was why Henry kept saying he was sorry when he thought she was Lizzie. Maybe Henry regretted not being able to protect Lizzie from what Brady and his friends did to her.

Emilia wanted to cry, but the tears wouldn't form. The thought that the minute she walked through those prison gates, she would possibly be facing the only person who knew what happened to Lizzie was almost consuming. What would she say to him? How would she feel seeing him? This man, Brady, may have killed Randel and hurt Lizzie out of hate. That would have meant that he was nothing more than a monster. Emilia had dealt with a lot of creepy people in her career, but she'd never had to stare into the eyes of a monster.

As she sat in a small room waiting for the guards to bring Brady in, she'd begun to have second thoughts. She started to feel that perhaps everyone was right, maybe she should just leave this alone. The emotions that she was feeling became almost overwhelming. Her heart pounded louder with each passing second. Then the cell doors opened and in an orange jumpsuit was this scruffy, skinny, white man that looked as if years of drug abuse had raged a war with his physical appears.

The guard sat Brady down across from Emilia and handcuffed his hands to the table. When the guard left,

Emilia couldn't think of the words she wanted to say. She just stared at him trying to see if there was any semblance of a caring human being. But his face was cold and detached. The look he gave her sent chills through her body.

"Who the hell are you?" Brady asked.

"My name is Emilia, and I'm a Reporter."

"What do you want with me?"

"I want to talk to you about what happened in Arbor in 1990." Emilia leaned in so that Brady would know that she was serious.

Brady sat back in his chair and looked around nervously, "I ain't got nothing to say about that."

"I think you do. I think you and your friends committed murder that night. I'm here to help you Brady, but I need to know what happened."

"I ain't kill nobody."

"Then you know who did. One of your friends you were with perhaps?'

"Lady I ain't kill nobody and don't know who did," Brady's face grew tense.

"I can tell this is weighing on you. Why?"

"Why?" Brady leaned in closer, "People called me and my momma all kinds of names. Them black folk damn near tried to run her out of town. My momma been living in Arbor all her life and didn't nobody give a damn about that. I tried to tell the cops then, and I'll tell you again I ain't kill nobody."

"Then tell me what happened that night."

"Why the hell should I?"

"Because I'm the only one around who cares enough to listen."

Brady looked at Emilia for a long time. He sat back in his chair and sucked his teeth. Emilia could see his swastika tattoo on his forearm, and it made the hair on the back of her neck stand up. The thought that Lizzie had to be subjected to such level of hate angered Emilia.

"I lived with my daddy two towns over, and that's where I went to high school. I would come visit my momma, but Arbor wasn't my kind of place." Brady started to explain.

"Because there were a lot of black people there?" Emilia asked.

"Guess you can say that. Anyway, we came down that night for a football game which we lost. On our way home a group of us saw the Arbor football team heading into the woods, all happy and shit. Anyway, we follow them and got into it bit." Brady continued to explain.

"What do you mean got into it?"

"Talking trash, a little shoving. Them black boys gave as good as they got."

"A witness saw a white kid coming out the woods battered and bruised."

"He didn't get that way from us. All the white kids left when the argument started. Guess they didn't want no parts of it."

"So then what happened?"

"Nothing. Someone yelled that they were going to get the Sheriff and we took off. I didn't know anyone had died until the next morning when the Sheriff came knocking at my door. The Son-of-a-Bitch had it out for me from the start. He was hell bent on proving that I did it. When everything went crazy, my daddy told my momma to get away from Arbor and that crazy ass Sheriff Roberts, but she refused to leave her home. I ain't been back, not even after that crazy Sheriff left and his son Caleb took over. They all had it out for me."

"Maybe because you hung with a biker gang who were known for their hateful behavior," Emilia said.

Brady chuckled, "We just had some fun."

"If you and your friends didn't do anything, then how did you get Lizzie's personal information?" Emilia asked.

"What are you talking about?" Brady shrugged.

"I met a woman named Elizabeth Potter. Only she wasn't the real Elizabeth Potter. She said she got the information from a biker gang called the Devil's Skull. Those were who you were in the woods with that night, wasn't it?"

Brady pressed his lips together and looked around the room as if he was trying to see who was listening.

"Yeah, that's who I was with," he answered.

"And you want me to believe that you had nothing to do with Lizzie's disappearance?" Emilia asked.

"I sure do because I didn't," Brady said. "I found those things in the woods. Lizzie had taken off long before I did. I have no idea where the hell she went."

"Why would she have her personal information in the woods?"

"How the hell should I know?" Brady replied. "I found a big black duffle bag on the ground filled with women's clothes and a wallet with her ID, social security card, and a couple of dollars. I didn't see her, so I figured I'll just take it."

Emilia sat up straight in the chair. What Brady was telling her didn't make sense. Why would Lizzie have a duffle bag filled with clothes?

"Thank you," Emilia said as she got up to leave.

"Wait a minute, I thought you was going to help me?" Brady called out to her.

"Fortunately, I can't," Emilia responded as the cell doors open for her to walk through.

Emilia wasn't sure if Brady was telling her the truth. But his story seemed believable enough. If Brady was telling the truth, then she was back at square one with no other suspects to investigate. She was sure that Brady and his biker friends had something to do with Lizzie's disappearance, but things didn't seem so clear anymore.

On her way back to Arbor, she started to put the puzzle together. As best as she could guess, Lizzie was a part of the group who went to celebrate that night. Maybe when Brady and his friends showed up, she took off and ran into Randel. Why Randel was in the woods that night is something that Emilia couldn't figure out. If Olive was right and someone called him, then there had to be a reason. Maybe someone was after Randel and Lizzie stumbled on it as she was running from Brady and his friends. But Emilia couldn't figure out who would have been after Randel. Everyone said that he was as straight as they came.

Emilia noticed that she was coming up to the woods where everything happened. It was dark by then, but Emilia had to take another look at those woods. She thought that if she could trace Lizzie's steps, then maybe something would seem clearer. She reached the clearing where the kids would have entered that night. Emilia parked her car and got out. She had a flashlight in the glove compartment of her car, which she took with her. She walked through the bushes, shining the flashlight ahead of her, and saw the area where the kids would have been hanging out before Brady and his friends interrupted. The scenic views were beautiful. It was secluded, quiet, and a perfect place for teens.

Emilia walked around the area for a while trying to figure out which way Lizzie would have run. She knew that there was a path from Lizzie's house to the woods and it would stand to reason that Lizzie would have been headed in that direction. Emilia just didn't know the woods well enough to know which direction that was. She started to walk further into the woods but then she heard a noise behind her that sounded like an engine starting.

Emilia turned around quickly only to be blinded by the headlights of what looked like a motorcycle. The engine roared louder and then the motorcycle started to come right towards Emilia at a high speed. Emilia took off running as fast as she could weaving through the trees and bushes, but the motorcycle kept coming. Emilia found a large rock and tried to hide behind it, but the motorcycle jumped right over, turned and started coming again. Emilia grabbed a large branch and waited for the motorcycle to get closer then she took a swing which caused the driver of the motorcycle to swerve on its side. Emilia didn't wait around to see what happened to the driver she took off running again.

She found herself by the cliff overlooking the river. She slowed down from running to see where she was going. But she had dropped her flashlight and couldn't see much. Before she could make a move, the motorcycle was back. This time coming much fast and Emilia was trapped between the cliff and the motorcycle. The motorcycle had her corner, and without thinking Emilia leaped over the cliff rolling down the cliff and landing on some bushes and rocks a few feet below. She turned her head in pain and looked up to see a hazy figure standing at the top of the cliff. Then the figure was gone and so was the sound of the motorcycle.

Emilia's whole body was in severe pain, and she could feel something wet dripping from her head. Emilia knew she couldn't stay where she was. She mustered up enough strength to pull herself back up to the top of the cliff, but she couldn't go any further. She was just about to lose consciousness when she heard someone yelling her name. She recognized Sheriff Caleb's voice, but she couldn't yell back. All she could do was moan, "Help. Help me."

Sheriff Caleb got to the cliff and saw Emilia laying there with her feet dangling off the cliff. He ran up to her "Emilia! Dear God." Sheriff Caleb picked Emilia up in his arms, holding on to her tightly. "I got you. Just hold on Emilia, I got you."

22

Emilia woke up to the sound of a beeping heart monitor and a blinding bright light. She tried to lift her arm to shield her eyes, but her arm felt heavy and weighted down. She moaned and tried to move, but her body was sore and felt bruised. She tried lifting her head but got dizzy.

"Hey, relax," Sheriff Caleb said as he stood over her and held her hand.

"Where am I?" Emilia asked.

"In the hospital," Sheriff Caleb responded. "Do you remember what happened?"

"Um… someone ran me off the trail. I fell over the cliff," Emilia said.

"How did you get back up?" Sheriff Caleb asked.

"I pulled myself up," Emilia answered.

"Did you see who it was or do you have any idea who it may be?" Sheriff Caleb continued to ask.

"No. I didn't see them." Emilia's vision was finally getting clear, and she could focus her eyes on Sheriff Caleb. "Thank you for saving me."

"It was my pleasure. But I told you to stay out of those woods at night," Sheriff Caleb said.

"I just had to take another look around," Emilia replied.

"Well, you better get some rest for now. You're pretty banged up, but the doctor said you didn't break anything, just gonna feel pretty sore for a while."

Emilia laid back and tried to close her eyes but her hospital room door swung open, and Chanel came running in with Sam following close behind her.

"Oh my God Em! Are you alright?" Chanel said running to Emilia's bedside to give her a hug.

"Be careful, be careful. I'm fine just a little bruised," Emilia replied.

"Are you sure?" Sam asked.

"I'm sure," said Emilia.

"I knew I shouldn't have let you come here by yourself," Sam told her.

"No, really everything is fine," Emilia said. "How did you guys know?"

"I phoned Ms. Chanel," Sheriff Caleb answered.

"That's Sha-nel," Chanel corrected.

"My apologies ma'am," Sheriff Caleb said to Chanel then turned his attention back to Emilia. "I figured you'll need folks around to take care of you."

"How did you know who to call?" Emilia asked Sheriff Caleb.

"Well, I guess you're not the only detective around here, are you?" Sheriff Caleb replied. "I'll leave you folks alone."

"Thank you, Sheriff," Emilia said with a smile.

After Sheriff Caleb left, Chanel and Sam sat down next to Emilia and listened as Emilia explained everything that's been happening. She saw the worried looks on their faces when she talked about the motorcycle running her off the cliff. She could see the concern all over Chanel.

"Someone is trying to kill you Em, and we need to get you out of here," Chanel said.

"I don't think the person was trying to kill me. I think they were trying to scare me," Emilia replied.

"Scare you from what?" Sam asked.

"From finding out what happened to Lizzie and who killed Randel," Emilia answered.

"Well, you're officially scared. So as soon as the doctor releases you, we are getting our asses out of Mayberry, and back to the calm streets of New York City, these people are crazy," proclaimed Chanel

"Chanel, the fact that someone came after me means I'm getting close. I can't leave now, I won't," Emilia said.

"I'm afraid to say it but I think she's right. Someone wants you off this issue and quick. Any idea who that is?" Sam said.

"I don't know. But I don't think that it's a coincidence that it happened right after I left the jail," Emilia replied.

"You think someone didn't like the fact that you went to see Brady?" Sam asked again.

"Maybe," Emilia replied.

"You guys sound crazy. Someone is trying to kill her. She needs to leave now." Chanel demanded.

"I agree," Donavan walked in and stood in the door way.

Emilia couldn't help but smile at the sight of him. She thought he was gone for good, and that she had destroyed any chance of them. But there he was. Donavan walked in and stood by her bedside and gently grabbed hold of her hand.

Chanel motion to Sam for them to leave. They walked outside and closed the door behind them. While standing outside of Emilia's door, Chanel noticed Sheriff Caleb having a very secret conversation with a doctor. She watched closely and tried to read their lips and expression, but for the life of her, she couldn't figure out what they were talking about. She tapped Sam and pointed his attention in that direction, but Sam didn't seem as alarmed by the conversation as Chanel was. He just shrugged his shoulders and went to sit down. Chanel kept a close eye on the conversation until it was over. Then she went and sat next to Sam.

Inside Emilia's hospital room, Donavan continued holding on to Emilia's hand as he sat on the chair next to her bed. Emilia was happy to see him, happier than she thought she would be. She still saw the love in Donavan's eyes. His smile still warmed her heart, and his touch still made her feel safe.

"So I hear you're running around playing amateur detective," Donavan chuckled.

"I guess," Emilia replied.

"May I ask what brought this on?" Donavan asked.

"Just trying to fix the broken pieces," Emilia answered.

Donavan ran his fingers across Emilia's face and smiled. He lifted her hand and gently kissed her fingers.

23

The next day, the doctors gave Emilia the all clear to leave the hospital. Chanel and Donavan wanted her to pack up and leave Arbor immediately, but Emilia said her work in Arbor was not done. She had to finish putting all the pieces together; she had to find out what happened to Lizzie. Sam agreed with her. He vowed to stay with her even if the other two didn't. He told Emilia that he had to do it for Henry. Sam had known ever since he was a little boy that something tormented Henry and he had to find out what that was.

Chanel insisted that Emilia at least go back to bed and breakfast to get some rest after just being released from the hospital, but Emilia refused. She wanted to go back to the woods and see if there were any clues as to who ran her off the cliff. Emilia's determination was too strong for the others to compete with. So all of them went with her to the woods.

Because the weather had been pretty good the last few days, the tracks from the motorcycle were still pretty visible. They walked around it for a while trying to figure out where it started from, but it was hard to determine.

"There's too many back and forth," Sam said as he bent down to get a closer look at the track.

"Didn't someone die in these woods?" Chanel asked as she looked around nervously.

"Really Chanel?" Emilia replied.

"Those bushes over there looked disheveled," Donavan said as he went over to look at them. "It looks like there's enough space to hide a motorcycle. EM, could someone have been waiting for you?'

"I don't see how. I came straight from the jail here. No one knew I was coming," Emilia replied.

"Maybe someone followed you? Did anyone know you were going to the jail?" Sam asked.

"I did tell Sheriff Caleb that I wanted to go, but I don't think he knew that I went," Emilia said.

"See Sam, I said that there was something about that Sheriff guy. I mean he's cute and all but there's something,

I can't put my fingers on it, but I know there's something," Chanel said.

"What are you talking about?" Emilia asked.

"Chanel saw Sheriff Caleb talking to a doctor in the hospital," Sam explained.

"So?" Donavan replied.

"Oh God Donavan, you just miss all the clues," Chanel replied.

"What clues am I missing Chanel?" Donavan asked frustrated.

"He's the one who found her here. He brought her to the hospital, then he's all close and secretive with a doctor. Come on guys, something is not right," Chanel explained.

"I never got that vibe from him," Emilia said.

"I didn't either. If he was after Emilia, he wouldn't have called us when she got hurt," Sam said.

"Ok fine. Don't say I didn't warn you," Chanel said.

"Actually, Chanel may be on to something," Donavan said as he looked around the woods.

"What do you mean?" Emilia asked.

"Well, these are some pretty big woods," Donavan said.

"So?" Emilia asked.

"So, how did he know you were here and where to find you?" Donavan asked again.

While they were talking, Sam had been following the tracks with his eyes. He saw one that wasn't disturbed that lead straight through some bushes. He began to walk towards the bushes.

"Where does this lead?" he asked Emilia.

"I'm not sure," Emilia replied.

They all walked towards the bushes and spread them apart and walked through them. The tracks from the motorcycle ended at another set of bushes that were mixed in with tall trees. Sam pulled the bushes apart and peeked through them. Then he turned around with a confused look on his face.

"Well, what do you see?" Chanel asked impatiently.

"Follow me," Sam said as he walked through the bushes.

On the other side was a sidewalk on the main street in Arbor. Emilia looked around and could see the courthouse, Sheriff's office, and the café.

"How could someone ride a motorcycle in the middle of town and no one not see anything?" Donavan asked.

"It seems to me that this town has been asleep for a long time," Sam replied.

Chanel looked around and saw Sheriff Caleb, a block down the street talking to a woman in what looked to be a heated conversation. "See there he is again talking all secretively to some woman."

"That's not some woman, that's Odessa," Emilia replied. "But why would they be arguing?"

Emilia immediately began to walk over to Sheriff Roberts and Odessa with the other three walking close behind. As she got closer, she could hear their voices getting louder, but their words didn't make much sense. Odessa motioned to Sheriff Caleb, who had his back to Emilia, that Emilia was quickly approaching. Sheriff Caleb turned around nervously as if he had been caught doing something wrong.

"Emilia. Should you be out the hospital so soon?" Sheriff Caleb asked.

"The doctors said I was good to go," Emilia replied.

"But I'm sure you should be taking it easy," Sheriff Caleb said.

Odessa stood there with an angry look on her face. She folded her arms and stared at Emilia. Emilia tried to ignore her, but the frustration of having to deal with Odessa treating her like she was an annoyance overwhelmed her.

"I'm fine. I still have work to do. Isn't that right Odessa?" Emilia said.

"Ain't got nothing else left here for you," Odessa said.

Sam stood beside Emilia to get a better look at Odessa. He had heard of his sister but had never seen her in person. She looked like their father. From her complexion to the curly disheveled jet black hair. He wanted to hug her. To tell her that no matter what happened they were family. He could feel Odessa's pain and wanted to make it all go away. He wanted to make things right, to fix whatever family bond that had been broken.

"I think there's a lot here for her, for us," Sam said.

"Who the hell are you?" Odessa asked.

"He's your brother," Emilia said.

Sam walked up to Odessa and held out his hand. "I'm Sam." But Odessa didn't budge.

She looked at Sam up and down and seem to grow even angrier. Sam could feel the hate and disgust pouring out of Odessa. He could sense her contempt for him. It seemed as if his existence touched a part of her spirit that was deeply damaged. She didn't even want to touch him, and she quickly turned her face so that she could no longer look at him.

Sheriff Caleb grabbed hold of Sam's hand and said, "It's a pleasure to meet you, Sam. Your father was a good man. I'm sorry for your loss."

"Thank you," Sam replied.

"Please. Henry wasn't shit. He went on down to New York City and got himself a brand-new family and didn't care about the one he left behind," Odessa finally turned to look into Sam's eyes. "But I guess he got the son he always wanted, now didn't he?"

"He talked about you all the time. He even tried to call. Staying away wasn't an easy decision for him Odessa," Sam said.

"Then why did he?" Odessa asked.

"That's what I would like to know," Emilia said.

Odessa turned to Sheriff Caleb and said, "Caleb you better make sure these folks get up out of town. We all don't need them here." Then she walked off in a fit of rage.

After Odessa left, Sheriff Caleb turned and looked at Emilia. "Something about you really gets under Odessa's skin."

"Because she doesn't want the truth to come out," Emilia said.

"And the truth is what you told me about who Lizzie was to you?" Sheriff Caleb asked.

"Yes. She's my birth mother. I just want to find out what happened to her," Emilia said.

Sheriff Caleb's face got sad and distracted. Something told Emilia that he wanted to believe her but was holding back for some reason. As if it was easier for him if Lizzie was dead, Sheriff Caleb nodded his head, turned, and walked away slowly.

"What do you think all that was about between them?" Sam asked Emilia.

"I have no idea," Emilia responded.

"This whole town is crazy," Chanel said.

"Come on Emilia, you should go rest. Besides, I'm starting to feed into Chanel's paranoia," Donavan said.

24

Emilia laid on her bed later that night, finally taking Chanel's advice to get some rest. She needed it. Between looking into Lizzie's disappearance and falling off a cliff, she was exhausted. Her body was still in pain, she still had minor scratches to her face, and her right hand was wrapped securely with a white Ace bandage to support her sprained wrist.

Emilia felt beaten but not defeated. She knew that somewhere in Arbor, someone knew the truth about what happened to Lizzie and she knew that someone was Odessa. Odessa wasn't shocked when she said she was Lizzie's daughter. To Emilia, that meant that Odessa knew that Lizzie had a child, and if Odessa knew that, it means Odessa knew that Lizzie didn't die that night in the woods. But what Emilia couldn't figure out was why Odessa wanted to keep that a secret.

There had to be a reason to why Odessa held on to this secret for so long and why she seemed so adamant about keeping it. If Lizzie was hurt in the woods and she wanted to hide, why would she still be hiding? Brady was in jail, and it had been so many years later.

Emilia thought about what Brady had told her. He was adamant that he didn't do anything, but Emilia still didn't know whether to believe him. From what Emilia understood about that night, it was chaotic, and there were other boys there besides Brady. Emilia wondered if one of those boys had left the group and maybe followed Lizzie. It would stand to reason that as the fight brook out, Lizzie would take off running back into the woods, after all, there was a trail from the woods right to her backyard. Maybe before Lizzie could get home, someone got to her first. Maybe Randel interrupted, and the person killed him. Maybe Lizzie ran and kept on running.

There were too many thoughts running through Emilia's head making it hard for her to sleep. She needed answers. Who killed Randel? Who scared Lizzie off? But most importantly, where was Lizzie?

There was one person that stuck in Emilia's head. Olive had said a witness saw a boy coming out from the woods looking like he had been in a fight. Brady said he didn't know who that was and neither he nor his friends had been in a fight. So who was the boy? And who did he fight? Emilia knew she had to find out who that boy was. He had to be the key to figuring out what happened that night.

Emilia rolled over to her side. The thought of what Lizzie must have gone through that night washed over her overwhelmingly. She hadn't stopped to consider how scared Lizzie must have been or how horrifying that night was for her. Emilia closed her eyes in pain, trying to imagine Lizzie at that moment. Tears filled her eyes, and her body grew cold.

Before Emilia could fully breakdown, there was a soft knock at her door. She sat up slightly, wiping the tears from her eyes, and told the person to come in. The door slowly opened and in walked Donavan. His smile subsided Emilia's tears, and his presence made her feel safe. She sat up in the bed to greet him.

"How are you feeling?" Donavan asked as he sat on the edge of her bed.

"I'm better, I think," Emilia replied.

"That's good. So, should we talk about what happened with us or is it too soon?" Donavan smiled.

"I really am sorry Don," Emilia said.

"No. I think I pushed you for more than you were ready for. I made you run, and for that, I'm the one who's sorry," Donavan said.

"Can we get past this?" Emilia asked.

"I don't know Em. I still love you more than anything. But…" Donavan stopped mid-sentence.

"But what?" Emilia asked.

Donavan opened his mouth to speak, but Chanel came in the room flinging the door open and startling Donavan and Emilia.

"That cute but suspicious Sheriff is downstairs. He says he needs to see you now," Chanel explained.

Emilia hurriedly got out of bed and made her way downstairs with Donavan and Chanel following close behind. They found Sheriff Caleb holding a box in his hand. The box didn't seem heavy but it was clear that there was something in it. Sam stood at the bottom of the steps leaning against the wall, he gave the other three a shoulder shrug, indicating that he didn't know what was going on.

Cecilia stood next to Sheriff Caleb looking disturbed. As soon as Emilia came down the stairs, she looked at Sheriff Caleb with concern in her eyes.

"Don't do this Caleb. Don't open this up again," Cecilia pleaded.

"I have to Cecilia," Sheriff Caleb said.

"No, you don't. Just let the dead stay dead," Cecilia said.

"Maybe they ain't dead Cecilia," Sheriff Caleb responded.

"Y'all talking crazy. I be in my room. I don't want any parts of this," Cecilia shook her head and left.

Sheriff Caleb motioned for Emilia and the other three to follow him in the dining room. As they gathered around the table, Sheriff Caleb put the box on the table. He held his hand over it and looked at Emilia.

"This ain't me saying I believe you. This just in case what you're saying is true," he said. "I called my daddy, and he told me where to find the evidence from that night. It was all achieved in a storage facility just outside of town."

Emilia wanted to question him as to why it wasn't with the other evidence, the ones belonging to Randel that were stored in the basement of the library. But she wanted to see what he was going to show them and didn't want to risk him becoming defensive.

Sheriff Caleb emptied out the box. Out of it came an old notebook, photos of the crime scene, and one foot of a woman's bloody sneaker wrapped in a clear plastic bag. Sheriff Caleb stared at the sneaker.

"All that was left of Lizzie was this bloody sneaker," Sheriff Caleb said.

Emilia gently rubbed her hand over the sneakers. Donavan placed his arm around her and held her tightly.

"Did they run a DNA test?" Emilia asked.

"Everything you need to know about the investigation is in this book." Sheriff Caleb held up the old notebook and laid it in front of Emilia. He then took one last look at her and left.

Emilia picked up the notebook and sat down. She began to read it, engrossing herself in every syllable. She was trying to find something she didn't already know. But it all seemed to be the same thing. There was a lot of talk about Brady and the biker gang. It was clear the Sheriff was sure that they had something to do with it.

The notebook said that the Sheriff had questioned Brady several times but got nowhere. Brady wouldn't give the names of the other boys who were with him, and he insisted that they did nothing wrong. There was no mention of any other suspects.

Emilia tossed the notebook down in frustration, "There's nothing there," she proclaimed.

Donavan picked it up and began to read it as he walked around the room. Chanel comforted Emilia whose eyes were still focused on Lizzie's one bloody shoe. Sam tried to examine the photos hoping that he would be able to gain some psyche in the mind of the person who could have done it.

From the photos of Randel's body, Sam could see that he was bruised maybe from some sort of fight or from being beaten. But there was nothing more that stood out to him. Nothing that would help him point to one person or another.

"This is interesting," Donavan said.

"What?" Emilia asked,

Donavan turned the notebook on its side and squinted his eyes slightly, "There's a small note here."

"What does it say?" Emilia asked as she got up and walked over to Donavan.

"It says Oldman Atkins claims to have seen Henry Potter carrying what looked to be a body into his house. No lead. Atkins probably drunk," Donavan read.

"Who's Oldman Atkins?" Chanel said.

"I don't know," Emilia replied as she searched her mind for some answers.

Then she took off and began banging on Cecilia's door. Cecilia answered, shocked at Emilia's behavior.

"Who's Oldman Atkins?" Emilia demanded.

"What?" Cecilia asked.

"I know you want me to leave Lizzie to rest in peace. But Cecilia, she was your best friend. What if she isn't dead? What if she's out there somewhere and needs our help?" Emilia pleaded.

"I can't tell you what happened that night. After those boys came looking for a fight, I went one way, and Lizzie went the other. I carry that with me every single day." Tears fell down Cecilia's face. She folded her arms trying to hang on to herself. "Oldman Atkins was the town drunk. He lived next door to Lizzie and her family. Lizzie liked him, and he liked her. She was always bringing him food or clothes or something."

"Where is he now?" Emilia asked.

"He's dead. He died a few years back," Cecilia answered.

"Would you trust what he said?" Emilia asked again.

"Oldman Atkins? No. he lived his whole life in a bottle. Towards the end of his life, he kept hollering about seeing Lizzie in the woods."

"Where in the woods?" Emilia asked.

"I don't know. No one took him seriously." Cecilia replied.

Emilia turned around and looked excitedly at Sam, Donavan, and Chanel. Her face had lightened up. Sam smiled back at her sensing exactly what she was thinking.

"Cecilia, how big are those woods?" Sam asked.

"I don't know. I guess if you cross the river it could take you all the way to the other town," Cecilia replied.

"I would think that's big enough for someone to live for years and not be found," Emilia said to Donavan, Sam, and Chanel.

She was ready to go back into the woods right then and there and search every inch of it. But Donavan convinced them to wait until daylight. He figured they should have light on their side if they were going to search for a needle in a haystack.

25

The next morning, Emilia came down the stairs to find Sam and Chanel at the table waiting for her. Cecilia had just begun to cook something for them to eat but they were too anxious to follow the new clue they had been given the night before.

Emilia looked around and didn't see Donavan. She asked where he was but no one seemed to know. She thought that he might still be asleep and didn't want to go. She was disappointed. Finding out about what happened to Lizzie was important to her and she'd hoped it was important to Donavan.

But she knew she couldn't fault him. After all she'd put him through it was only right that she cut him a break. If he didn't want to help with the search for Lizzie, she had to respect that. Besides, a part of Emilia wanted to make this journey alone. She figured that if Oldman Atkins was right and he had seen Lizzie in the woods after she was pronounced dead, then she still may be in the woods. She didn't want to scare Lizzie by having her face a bunch of strangers. Yet, she knew that Sam would not stay behind and that Chanel's curiosity would not let her stay either.

"Are you ready?" Sam asked Emilia.

"Yeah I think so," Emilia replied.

"Are ya'll not going to eat before ya'll leave?" Cecilia asked.

"I'm not really hungry," Emilia said.

"Neither am I," Sam replied.

"Well –" Chanel began to say.

"Chanel." Emilia looked at her with a stern face.

"How are we going to go hiking without food in our stomachs?" Chanel asked.

"We'll be fine. But you can stay if you want," Emilia replied.

"No, I'm coming," Chanel said conceding.

"Y'all are about the craziest bunch I ever seen. If you're gonna chase ghost, you outa do it on a full stomach," Cecilia said as she walked back into the kitchen.

"I agree," Chanel grumbled under her breath. Emilia shot her a mean look, "What? I'm coming, I'm coming."

When they went outside, they saw Donavan coming up to the house with a backpack over his shoulders. For a moment Emilia thought that Donavan was packed and ready to head back to New York. Disappointment began to set in on her face. She'd spent years keeping Donavan at arm's length, but now she really wanted him there, holding her hand and telling her that everything was going to be alright. She had sent Donavan so many mixed messages throughout the years that she wasn't sure what her true feelings were towards him. All she knew at that moment was that she wanted him with her.

"Hey, guys," Donavan said as he reached them.

"Where did you go?" Chanel asked.

"Just had to take care of some things," Donavan said. He took the backpack from off his shoulder and opened it, "I figured if we're going deep into the wood, then we need some things."

He pulled out a rope, a first aid kit, bottles of water, a small fishing knife, and a map. Donavan stood tall and looked at the expressions on the faces of the other three. Sam nodded his head in agreement as the girls took mental note of all that Donavan had shown them.

"Do you happen to have any food in there?" Chanel asked.

Donavan took out a snack bar and handed it over to her. A smile of gratitude immediately came across Chanel's face, and she was now ready for whatever the others had planned.

"Alright, let's go," Sam said as he walked to the car.

Donavan put everything back into the backpack and tossed it over his shoulders. Emilia looked at him as she walked passed, not knowing what to say.

The four of them got to the opening of the woods and entered the woods with Emilia leading the way. They walked through every inch of the woods even up to the trail leading to Odessa's house. But there was nothing; they didn't even know what they were looking for.

They reached the cliff overlooking the river. Donavan took the map and began to read it. Chanel leaned up against a tree exhausted. Sam and Emilia looked around trying to figure out what would be their next move.

"It seems like across the river there's more woods that leads to the other town," Donavan said.

"Yeah, that's what Cecilia said," Sam said as he stretched his eyes to see to the other side of the river.

"Well, how do we get over there?" Emilia asked.

Donavan and Sam both began to look at the map. Emilia walked to the edge of the cliff, rested her hand on her forehead to protect her eyes from the sun and tried to get a better look at the other side of the river.

"Why don't we use the old broken-down bridge over there?" Chanel said pointing to a bridge in the far distant.

"Chanel, you are awesome," Emilia said.

"I know," Chanel said with a smirk.

They quickly made their way to the bridge. But when they got there, they realized that the bridge was rotted and decayed. It looked as if no one had used it in years. Sam put one foot on the bridge and shook it gently. It was very wobbly. Sam took his foot off it and turned to the others.

"Ok, I'll go first. You ladies come after and Donavan you come last. Let's go slow," Sam instructed.

They did as Sam instructed and slowly walked across the bridge at times feeling as if the whole thing would collapse under them.

Soon they reached the other side. Chanel yelled out, "Thank God!" as Donavan read the map and try to figure out which directions they should go. He pointed them in the direction straight ahead, and they made their way through the trees and bushes

This side of the river was not as clear and open as the other side. It was hard to see where they were and what was surrounding them. They walked until they reached what they believed to be a clearing. They made their way through the trees and there waiting for them was an old cabin.

Emilia walked up ahead and stopped. She turned and looked back at the others. Then she put her attention back on the cabin. Her stomach balled up in knots. Suddenly the thought came to her that Lizzie may be in the cabin. Emilia whispered "Lizzie" and then ran up to the cabin.

She ran to the front door and was about to knock but the door opened on its own. By then the other three had caught up to her. Emilia pushed the door slowly not knowing what she would find inside. There was nothing. Inside the cabin looked abandoned. As if no one had lived there ever. It was dusty and molded and filled with cobwebs.

Emilia stood in the middle of the cabin as anger crept up on her. It was another dead-end. Another place where Lizzie was not. Sam and Chanel began to look around. Donavan came up behind Emilia and put his arms around her.

"I'm sorry Emilia," he said.

"I really thought this was it. I thought she would be here waiting for me to find her," Emilia replied.

"We're getting close Em," Donavan said.

"Are we?" Emilia asked walking away from Donavan's embrace and turned to face him. "Look at this place. Was she ever even here? I feel like I'm running in circles and this damn town wants to hold on to what ever happened that night so tightly. At this point, I should just let them and go back to New York."

"The Emilia I know is not a quitter," Donavan said.

"Donavan, she is not here and I'm starting to think that maybe Lizzie did die that night. Maybe she's not even my mother, and this has all been some sick joke," Emilia said.

"But she may have been, and you may have been here as well," Sam said holding up a dusty pink baby blanket.

Emilia grabbed the blanket out of Sam's hand and held it tightly. "Where did you find this?" Emilia asked him.

"There's a room back there," Sam replied.

Emilia walked in the direction Sam was pointing. She found a bedroom with a dirty old bed and one window that was caked in dust. She looked around the room and tried to imagine Lizzie being there. But she wasn't, and Emilia was again left wondering where she was and how this old cabin deep in the woods fit in to what happened to Lizzie.

26

"Em, are you ready to get out of here?" Donavan asked as he watched Emilia standing in the empty bedroom lost in thought.

They had been there for almost an hour and had found nothing that would bring them closer to finding Lizzie. The others had left Emilia alone with her thoughts as they searched the area around the cabin. But now it was time to go. There was nothing else there for them to find.

Emilia felt connected to that bedroom. Something about it seemed familiar as if she had been there before. It was dusty and smelled of mold, but Emilia felt at home. She didn't want to leave. It was the only place she felt truly connected to Lizzie. It was as if leaving meant leaving Lizzie behind and she couldn't bear to do that.

Nevertheless, she had to. She had to continue the journey to find Lizzie. Emilia wrapped her arms around her waist and fought back the tears. She walked up close to the bed and wanted to place her hands on it, but its dirty appearance prevented her from doing so.

Emilia turned her head towards Donavan and smiled. She had finally built up enough strength to walk out of the room. Emilia turned her body to leave, but her foot kicked an object that was under the bed. The object swept from under the bed and stopped at Donavan's feet.

"What is that?" Emilia asked.

"It looks like a book," Donavan said as he blew the dust off it.

Emilia took the book from Donavan and looked it over. It was an old romance novel. The front cover was designed with a beautiful young couple who looked completely in love. Emilia read the back description, and the story was about forbidden love. Emilia lifted her head and looked at Donavan with light in her eyes.

"The main character's name is Emilia," she said.

Donavan smiled at her. Emilia gently ran her fingers across the cover of the book. She tightly gripped it in her arms and walked out of the room.

Emilia and Donavan met Sam and Chanel outside the cabin. Emilia was still holding tightly to the book she found in the bedroom. Chanel looked at Emilia and the book in her arms asking, "What's that?"

"Something I found," Emilia replied.

"Was it Lizzie's?" Sam asked.

"I don't know," Emilia answered, "it just feels like I should hold on to it."

"So, what do you guys think?" Sam asked again.

"About what?" asked Emilia.

"Do you think this is where Lizzie ended up?"

Emilia turned and looked back towards where they came from. "Randel's body was found about two miles across the bridge. It's possible she took off and found this cabin like we did."

"But how long was she here?" Chanel asked.

"Long enough to have me at least," Emilia replied.

"Lizzie was a teenager, no way she would be able to go through nine months of pregnancy and give birth on her own," Donavan added.

"Yes, it is. A lot of teen girls carry a baby for nine months and give birth without anyone knowing," Chanel said.

"But someone did know," Emilia said.

"My dad," Sam added.

"Either Henry brought Lizzie here or found her here," Emilia said.

"Maybe he found her," Donavan said, "there was a big search for Lizzie, right? Maybe Henry came out this way searching for her and found her in this cabin."

"Then why not tell people she was alive and that he had found her?" Chanel asked.

"Maybe Lizzie told him what happened in the woods and he figured it was safer for her to stay here," Emilia explained.

"Then whatever happened to Randel and Lizzie in the woods that night was so bad that my dad had to let everyone think she was dead," Sam said.

"Everyone except Odessa and maybe she and Lizzie's mother too," Emilia said.

"Lizzie being alive was their secret. It would explain why they had to get rid of the baby she had," Donavan said as he put his arms around Emilia.

"Yeah, in order not to let people know that Lizzie was alive, I had to go away," Emilia said somberly.

"The only question now is what happened after?" Sam asked, "how did my dad get a baby out of a small town without anyone seeing him?"

"Let me see that map," Emilia said to Donavan.

Emilia looked at every inch of that map, making the cabin's location the center point. She took one finger and ran it from where the cabin would be on the map all the way up then she stopped, lifted her finger and pointed straight ahead of her. "He didn't have to go back to Arbor. Straight that way is another town."

"You think he carried the baby through all those trees?" Chanel asked.

"Maybe he had help," Sam said.

"Yeah, maybe Odessa or their mother or maybe Lizzie," Emilia said.

"It would make sense that Henry took more than the baby away," Donavan said.

"Wait, you guys think Lizzie was with my dad when he went to New York?" Sam asked.

"I don't know," Emilia answered.

"Well, we can't stand here and try to figure it out. It'll be dark soon. Let's head back." Donavan said.

The four of them walked back the way they came. There was a still quiet among them. It was obvious that each of them was thinking about what they had discovered. The mystery of Lizzie had taken hold of each of them, and they all had to see it through.

27

They were sweaty and exhausted when they returned to the bed and breakfast. They walked through the door and met Cecilia standing behind the desk with an unemotional look on her face. Chanel walked in first and passed Cecilia giving her a wave and walking up the steps. Sam followed Chanel and greeted Cecilia with a smile and a wave.

Emilia and Donavan stood in front of the desk facing Cecilia. Cecilia looked them over and saw the messiness of their appearance. She smirked to herself and asked, "Are you guys done chasing ghost?"

Emilia placed the book from the cabin down on the desk and leaned on it, "Why does this bother you so much, Cecilia?"

"Because Lizzie was my best friend and she deserves to rest in peace." Cecilia looked down. Her eyes landed on the book from the cabin, "Where did you get that?"

"We found a cabin on the other side of the river in the woods. This was there," Donavan said.

Cecilia's face was frozen from shock. Tears filled her eyes as she ran her hand across the book. Her brown face turned rosy. Emilia watched Cecilia's expression become a desperate sense of loss.

"What's wrong Cecilia?" Emilia asked.

"This was Lizzie's favorite book. She loved it and must have read this book like a hundred times," Cecilia explained.

"The main character has my name," Emilia asked.

"Does it?" Cecilia asked.

"Best friends share everything. I mean Chanel is my best friend, there isn't anything she doesn't know about me," Emilia said as she stared intently at Cecilia.

"What are you getting at Emilia?" Cecilia responded.

"Who was Lizzie with in the woods that night?" Emilia asked.

"I told you I don't know what happened that night. Lizzie went one way, and I went the other," Cecilia said sounding frustrated.

"But that's just it. In the middle of the chaos, true best friends would never split up, unless they were sure that the other was safe. So why were you sure?" Emilia pressed. "Does it have something to do with this book? Was Lizzie seeing someone?"

Cecilia didn't speak. She just stared at that book with sadness in her eyes.

"Why did Lizzie love this book so much?" Emilia continued. The look on Cecilia's face convinced Emili that she was on to something.

"Because she…" Cecilia began to say but instantly looked up in fear and stopped herself.

Cecilia jerked her hand from the book and ran down the hall into her room. Emilia tried to run after her, but Donavan stopped her.

"Something is hurting her," Donavan said, "let's give her some space for now."

Emilia and Donavan went into Cecilia's den and sat down. Emilia was aware that Cecilia knew far more about Lizzie's life than she was willing to say. She may not have known about what happened to Lizzie that night, but Emilia was convinced that what Cecilia did know could help to fill in some of the gaps.

Donavan walked around the room looking at Cecilia's books as Emilia laid her head across the arm of the chair. Sam and Chanel came in, both looking fresh from a shower.

"Have you two been down here the whole time?" Chanel asked as she sat next to Emilia.

"Yup. We tried to talk to Cecilia, but that was a bust," Emilia said.

"Why? What happened?" Sam said.

"She knows about Lizzie's life. I just wish she would tell me," Emilia replied.

"You think she knows where Lizzie is?" Sam asked again.

"No. At least I don't think so. I believe her when she says she doesn't know what happened to Lizzie that night. But that doesn't mean she doesn't know what was going on with Lizzie up until then," Emilia explained."

"Like what?" Sam asked.

"Like if Lizzie had a boyfriend or if someone was bothering her. I think Cecilia knows all that, but she just won't talk to me," Emilia said.

"Does she know who you are?" Sam Continue to ask.

"I didn't tell. By the way, Sheriff Caleb responded to me, I figured I'll keep that little information to myself," Emilia said.

"Maybe you should tell her," Sam said.

"Why do you think she should?" Donavan asked.

"If Cecilia loved Lizzie as much as I think she did, then Lizzie's daughter is the only one that could get through to her," Sam said.

Sam looked at Emilia with his eyebrow raised.

"What, now?" Emilia asked.

"There's no time like the present," Sam said.

"You need back up?" Chanel asked.

"No, Emilia and Cecilia need this moment alone," Sam said, "but we'll be right here if you need us.

Emilia got up and slowly walked to Cecilia's door. She gently tapped on it nervously. Cecilia opened it and peeked through.

"Yes," Cecilia said.

"May I come in?" Emilia asked.

Cecilia opened the door and let Emilia into her room. Emilia walked in and turned to face Cecilia.

"I'm sorry for earlier," Emilia said.

"I just don't understand why this story, whatever it is, that you are writing about Odessa is so important that you would want to drag Lizzie up out of her grave," Cecilia said.

"I'm not writing a story about Odessa. I told you that," Emilia said.

"Well, I didn't believe you. Ever since Lizzie and Randel died, folks been trying to come in here and make some big whoop about it. Caleb has been protecting this town from all that mess. Don't know why he wants to stop now," Cecilia said.

"He doesn't have to protect Lizzie or her memory from me Cecilia I promise you. I just want to find out what happened to Lizzie that night," Emilia said.

"Why does it matter so much to you?" Cecilia asked.

"Because Lizzie was my birth mother," Emilia said.

"What?" Cecilia asked in shock. "That's not possible."

Cecilia walked over to her bed and sat down. Her face seemed to be stuck in a faraway place, and her eyes were searching her mind for answers.

"It's true Cecilia. That's how I know Lizzie didn't die that night because if she did, I wouldn't be here. Please help me, Cecilia. Tell me about Lizzie. Was someone bothering her? Maybe they attacked her in the woods that night. Maybe that's how she ended up pregnant with me. Please, Cecilia," Emilia pleaded.

Cecilia looked at Emilia and covered her mouth with both her hands. With tears streaming down her face she shook her head furiously.

"It can't be. It can't be," Cecilia repeated.

"It is. I'm Lizzie's daughter. Was she hurt that night? Before that night? Anything you could tell me? Did Henry-"

"No! No!" Cecilia got up and looked at Emilia in disbelief. "She was pregnant before that night. No one hurt her. She was in love. They wanted to run away together. To be a family."

Emilia smiled, and a look of relief came across her face. "Who was he?"

Cecilia looked away. "I can't, not now. Please leave my room. Please, Emilia. Please."

Cecilia gently pushed Emilia out of her room and locked the door behind her. Emilia could hear Cecilia sobbing from the other end. Emilia fell to the ground and buried her head in her lap.

<h1 style="text-align:center">28</h1>

The next morning, Emilia was gone before the others woke up. She had to go and see Sheriff Caleb and fill him in on what they'd found. She'd hoped that with the additional information maybe he'll believe her that Lizzie didn't die that night, maybe he'll open an official investigation into Lizzie's disappearance and that may put the pressure on Odessa to finally say what happened to Lizzie.

Although, after talking to Cecilia, Emilia began to wonder if she was wrong all along. Maybe Odessa didn't really know about Lizzie. Maybe Lizzie and whoever it was that she was in love with did run away to be a family after all, only without her. Maybe they left her with Henry and then took off.

Searching for what happened to Lizzie gave Emilia the hope that she wasn't abandoned because nobody wanted her but because of terrible circumstances. But now, Emilia was starting to think that Lizzie may have run off and left her behind. She had become afraid of the truth all over again.

But after all, she had gone through in Arbor, she needed to know what happened to Lizzie.

When Emilia reached Sheriff Caleb's office, he was sitting at his desk staring out of the window looking as if his mind was a million miles away. Emilia stood in his door way for a moment just staring at him. Then she finally said, "Sheriff."

Sheriff Caleb turned around and immediately stood up. He walked towards Emilia and looked her up and down. It was as if it was his first time seeing her. His face was emotionally stiff, his light brown eyes danced up and down her face, and slight beads of sweat dripped and rested on his alabaster skin.

"Are you alright Sheriff?" Emilia asked.

"Oh yes, yes I'm fine. How may I help you, Emilia?" Sheriff Caleb said as he stepped back and walked towards the window.

Emilia sat down and began to explain to Sheriff Caleb all that they had found. But it didn't appear that he was listening. He nodded his head routinely, but Emilia got the feeling that he hadn't heard a word she was saying. He didn't even realize that she had stopped talking. He had a far off look in his eye.

"Sheriff, did you hear me?" Emilia asked. "Lizzie had a boyfriend. But there was no mention of him in the notebook that your father had. We have to find him. I think that your dad was so focused on Brady and his friends that he totally missed another angle."

"Emilia, you've turned this town upside down," Sheriff Caleb said softly.

"That wasn't my intention Sheriff. I'm just trying to find out what happened to my birth mother," Emilia said.

Sheriff Caleb turned around strangely calm. He walked over to Emilia saying, "I need you to come with me."

"Where?" Emilia asked.

"You'll see," Sheriff Caleb said helping her out of the chair.

Back at the bed and breakfast, Sam and Chanel were sitting at the dining room table eating breakfast. Donavan came running down the stairs in a rush. He looked around as if he was searching for something or someone.

"What's going on?" Sam asked.

"Where's Emilia?" Donavan asked.

"I haven't seen her this morning," Chanel answered.

"Me neither. Why?" Sam said.

Donavan looked up and saw Cecilia come back into the dining room, "Cecilia have you seen Emilia?" Donavan asked.

"She left early this morning. I think she went to see Sheriff Caleb or at least she was headed in that direction, why?" Cecilia replied.

"We have to go," Donavan said to Sam and Chanel with panic in his eyes.

"Why?" Chanel asked.

"Come on, let's just go, now," Donavan demanded.

As they walked outside, Sam stopped Donavan. He needed to know what was going on with Donavan. Why he insisted that they leave so urgently.

“Wait,” Sam said. “What’s the rush?”

Donavan looked over Sam’s shoulder to make sure the door and windows were closed behind him.

“I sent Lizzie’s shoe to a friend who worked for the FBI and asked that he run a DNA test on it and he did,” Donavan explained.

“So, the police report said the blood belonged to Lizzie,” Sam said.

“Yeah, but I had a feeling, and I was right,” Donavan said.

“Right about what?” Chanel asked.

“Lizzie’s blood wasn’t on the shoe, but someone else was,” Donavan explained.

“Who?” Chanel asked.

“Sheriff Caleb,” Donavan answered.

Sam and Chanel looked at each other in astonishment. The information that Donavan was giving them was confusing.

"Wait a minute, how could Sheriff Caleb's blood have gotten on Lizzie's shoes?" Sam asked.

"Simple, he was there that night," Donavan answered.

"I knew there was something about him," Chanel said.

"Emilia's with him now, probably trying to convince him that Lizzie is still alive," Sam said.

"And Lizzie is the only witness from that night," Donavan said.

"We have to get to Emilia," Sam said.

Emilia got out of the car with Sheriff Caleb at the opening to the woods. His strange behavior filled her with nervous anxiety. She looked around, and they were the only two people around. Sheriff Caleb walked into the woods slightly and stopped. He turned towards her and waited for her to join him. Emilia hesitantly walked up to him, and they both entered the woods. Halfway in, Sheriff Caleb began to talk about his childhood in Arbor and his family. He told Emilia what it was like having a father who was a Sheriff of the town. He said that he never got married because he wanted a love like his parents had.

He stopped walking right at the edge of the cliff. Emilia stopped next to him as they looked out onto the river. Then Sheriff Caleb walked off by a set of trees and looked down on the ground.

"This is the exact spot where Randel's body laid," he said.

Emilia watched him in silence as his mind wandered off. He knelt down and took off his hat.

"That night plays in my mind like a broken record. It haunts me," he continued.

Emilia wanted to say something to ask him what it was about that night that haunted him, but she heard movement and the sound of someone making their way through the trees and bushes. Then finally the trees parted, and Odessa stepped through.

She seemed immediately angry at the sight of Emilia. She walked up to Sheriff Caleb and stood over him. He quickly stood up to face her.

"Why the hell am I here Caleb?" Odessa asked.

"What's going on?" Emilia asked, but both of them seemed not to be paying any attention to her.

"It's time for this to end Odessa that's why I texted you to meet me here. I know who she is. We are going to take care of this right now," Sheriff Caleb said.

Odessa looked at him defiantly with her arms folded. They stared at one another as if they were talking through their eyes.

"Can one of you please tell me what's going on?" Emilia asked.

Sheriff Caleb turned to her and placed his hand on his gun that was strapped to his waist. Emilia automatically felt alarmed. She took a step back but couldn't go any further because she was right at the edge of the cliff.

Odessa sighed, "I paid that fool of a boy good damn money to scare you out of this town, but you had to keep poking your nose where it didn't belong."

Emilia looked at Odessa in horror. She figured that it was Odessa who had something to do with what happened to her but hearing Odessa admit to it stirred up an uncontrollable anger in her. She wanted to rush Odessa, to scream and call her every name in the book, but both Odessa and Sheriff Caleb had her cornered. Her eyes kept jumping between the two, and her mind wondered how she would get out away from them.

Suddenly the thought ran across her mind that maybe everything she thought about that night may have been wrong. Nothing made sense. The only thing that was clear was that Odessa and Sheriff Caleb knew way more than what they had said.

"It's time for this to come to an end," Sheriff Caleb said with his one eye on Odessa and his hand still on his gun.

Emilia held her breath and looked down at the rushing river below. Fear quickly crept up on her. Then suddenly Sam, Donavan, and Chanel came running out of nowhere. Donavan stood in front of Emilia and shouted, "Get away from her!"

Emilia grabbed hold of Donavan's arms and let out a deep breath. "How did you guys know I was here?" she asked.

"Someone saw you and the Sheriff headed in this direction," Donavan said.

"Are you alright Em?" Chanel asked.

"Yeah, just glad to see you guys," Emilia replied.

"What is going on? Emilia isn't in any danger," Sheriff Caleb said.

"Odessa just admitted that she's the one who got someone to come after me that night," Emilia responded.

"What?" Sam asked in disbelief.

"She's not the only issue here," Donavan said.

"What do you mean?" Emilia asked.

Donavan looked at Sheriff Caleb and said, "Do you want to tell us how your blood got on Lizzie's shoes?"

"What are you talking about?" Emilia asked.

"I had a friend of mine run a DNA test on the blood found on Lizzie's sneakers, and it matched Sheriff Caleb Roberts' DNA."

Emilia looked at Sheriff Caleb with frantic disbelief, "What did you do?" she asked him.

Sheriff Caleb turned and faced Odessa. They locked eyes. Odessa unfolded her arms. Her defiant posture turned to compliance.

"It's time," Sheriff Caleb said.

PART III

Arbor 1990

29

When Lizzie and I were kids, we were the best of friends. We did everything together. You couldn't separate us. Daddy and mama were civil, but it was clear there was something wrong, but Lizzie and I didn't pay it no mind. It didn't affect us much. Daddy used to have us playing outside all the time. We were always running and jumping. Most of all he would always take us fishing. Lizzie and I loved going fishing with daddy.

Mama used to say that he always wanted a son but that well had run dry. She wasn't about to have another baby so that daddy could get his boy. So, Lizzie and I benefited. We got to spend a lot of time with daddy. Those were the good days.

When daddy wasn't with us, he was with Mr. Atkins. He lived next door, and he and daddy had been friends for years. Mama didn't want Mr. Atkins around because she said he could out drink the best of them. Mr. Atkins didn't have anything good to say about mama either. Most people didn't.

Mama was tough, some say mean. But wasn't nobody fool enough to mess with her. Mr. Atkins used to say that mama had a heart of stone. One day, I heard him tell daddy to keep us away from mama before we turn out just like her.

"Henry that woman of yours ain't no good," Mr. Atkins said.

"George, my wife is none of your business," Daddy replied.

"It sure is my business. I love those two little girls, but Bee will destroy them. Hell, she damn near about to destroy you. That woman ain't nothing but evil," Mr. Atkins said while putting a bottle of beer to his mouth.

"Go on and keep drinking George. Me and my girls are alright," Daddy told him.

Mama was tough, but I always felt like she did what she had to for the family. Mama always knew what was best. I never once questioned her. I trusted that she knew what she was doing. I reckon daddy did too, to some extent. He always followed along with whatever she said.

But he always told Lizzie and me that we should follow our own hearts. He wanted us to be bigger than Arbor. Mama said there wasn't bigger and I believed her, Lizzie didn't. Lizzie was always reading books about far off places and people doing incredible things. She read this book about New York, and she and daddy started talking about the lights and the people.

Lizzie must have talked about that for weeks. She used to get on my nerves about it. But I just ignored her. Lizzie's mind was always up in the clouds. Guess I tried to stay practical for the both of us.

Lizzie was a dreamer, and I think daddy loved that about her, at least he encouraged it. She had this pure soul. She was like one of those Disney princesses. You know the ones that could walk in the forest singing beautifully, and all the animals would come around bow at her feet. That was Lizzie, the real-life Disney princess.

I guess that would have made me the wicked witch or evil stepsister or something. That became clear to me one day when daddy took us fishing. Mr. Atkins came with us too. I think I was about twelve and Lizzie was ten.

We were having a pretty good time at first, even though we had gone almost the whole time without catching anything. But it was a good time. Then all of a sudden something was tugging on Lizzie's line. Daddy helped her pull her line out the water.

Lizzie had caught herself a fish. It wasn't a big fish or anything, but it was her first catch. Daddy laid the squirming fish into the bucket and picked Lizzie up in his arms with joy. Even Mr. Atkins was excited. But it seemed like they forgot I was there. That's the first time I felt invisible. Something got to me. I looked down at that fish squirming in that bucket, and I picked up a rock and slammed it right on the fish.

Lizzie was telling daddy she wanted to put the fish back before it died but by then it was too late, I'd already put it out of its misery. When they realized what I did, they were pissed.

Lizzie began to cry and daddy was comforting her. Mr. Atkins looked at me with hate in his eyes. Daddy came over to me and shook me by the arm.

"What did you do Odessa?" he asked.

"The fish was going to die anyway," I replied not understanding why everyone was all freaked out.

"That wasn't your place to do that," Daddy said.

Lizzie knelt down by the bucket and began to rub her hand on the fish as if it was going to magically come back to life. Daddy knelt down beside her and hugged her.

"I'm sorry Lizzie," Daddy said.

"Can we give it a funeral?" Lizzie asked.

"Why would you give a fish a funeral? It supposed to be dinner," I told them.

"Odessa!" Daddy yelled at me. "Come on baby." Daddy scooped up a teary eye Lizzie in his arm and began to walk off.

I didn't know what all the fuss was about. Mr. Atkins stayed behind and looked at me as if I had ended the world.

"You just like your mama girl," Mr. Atkins said, "I told Henry it would happen. One of you girls were going to be just like that damn Bee."

"It was just a fish," I said.

"Girl you don't get it," Mr. Atkins said shaking his head.

He walked off and left me standing there wondering why they were all so mad. After that, Lizzie didn't talk to me for days. She barely wanted to look at me. Mama was like me; she didn't get the big deal. She kept telling Lizzie to get over it, that it was just a fish, but that seemed to make Lizzie even more upset. She moped around for weeks. It wasn't until daddy came home with two gold fish that she perked up.

That was Lizzie. She thought everything was special. Everyone and everything meant something to this world. I guess me killing that fish made her think I had taken something special out this world. Guess that's why we were never the same after that.

30

Lizzie and I stopped hanging around each other much. A new girl, Cecilia, moved across the street and they became best friends. They did everything together. Lizzie didn't have much use for me. At first, I was fine with it. I had a friend too, Randel. He got me. He tried to make me feel like I didn't have to be something I was not.

We bonded over sci-fi movies. We could talk about anything. I grew to love Randel, but I wasn't really sure how he felt about me. I guess I was satisfied with him being my friend. Then we entered high school and Randel and I didn't spend much time together anymore. He became the smart kid that all the teachers adored, and I was just there.

Nobody bothered me, and I didn't bother anybody, it was bearable. That was until Lizzie got there. High school went from being bearable to the worst time of my life. Lizzie popped in through those doors and instantly became everyone's favorite.

She was smart, popular, and beautiful. People loved Lizzie, and I was in the shadows. I once walked down the hallway and heard some girls talking.

"I can't believe she's Lizzie's sister," one girl said.

"She's so weird," the other girl said.

"What is she even wearing?" another girl responded.

They were right. I was weird. I dressed in all black and walked with my head down. No one cared to ask if I was okay. No one bothered to see why. Daddy only cared about Lizzie and mama thought weakness was unacceptable.

I had to sit on the sideline and watch my little sister be everything I wasn't. I remember Lizzie and I were coming home from school. Lizzie was walking ahead of me with Cecilia, and I just followed behind watching them. We reached Mr. Atkins house, and he was sitting on his porch drunk as usual. Lizzie ran up to him and gave him a hug. She cleaned up the area around him and gave him the rest of her uneaten lunch. Then she left with Cecilia.

I went to the porch and stood over Mr. Atkins. He lifted his head and looked at me. He gave me the same look he did the day I killed that fish.

"Well if it isn't the evil sister," he said.

"Says the town drunk," I replied.

"Girl you something mean like your mama," he said again. "You ain't never gonna be no Lizzie."

"I don't wanna be Lizzie," I told him.

"Yeah, you do. She's kind with a good heart. You, you got your mama's heart, all stone," he said. "You can't get to her. You and your mama can't destroy her no matter how hard you try," he replied.

"You sound crazy old man," I said to him.

He just kept staring at me and taking a drink from his bottle. I snatched the bottle from him poured it out.

"It's time to sober up old man," I said laughing.

Mr. Atkins tried to jump off the porch and grab his liquor bottle out my hand, but he stumbled and fell. The sight of him falling and hearing him yelling to give him back his bottle amused me and I couldn't help but let out a loud laughter.

Lizzie and Cecilia came running back. Lizzie grabbed the bottle out my hand before I could finish wasting it out.

"What are you doing Odessa?!" Lizzie yelled.

"Oh, like he needed another drink," I said to her.

Lizzie helped Mr. Atkins to his feet and sat him back on the porch. She gave him the bottle back and said to him, "I'm sure Odessa didn't mean nothing by it. Mr. Atkins."

"Yes, she did. She got her mama's heart," he said looking at me with contempt.

I smiled and walked away. But I really wanted to cry. Lizzie was the good one, and that was never going to change. Mr. Atkins was right. I was the evil sister. The weird one who didn't seem to fit as Lizzie's sister.

31

Ain't nothing worse than being the big sister to the perfect little sister. Lizzie was everyone's golden child. Everyone thought Lizzie walked on water and I was just some sideshow I reckon. Folks didn't even know I existed half the time. I could walk in a room, and no one would know I was there. But Lizzie, oh beautiful and perfect Lizzie, she would walk in that same room, and everyone would fall to her feet.

I kinda have to admit, some parts of me admired her too. She was everything I was not. I guess Mr. Atkins was right in some way; I did want to be Lizzie; at least know what it was like being her.

I took to following her around, just to see what it was about her that made her so perfect. I listened to her conversations and watched her and her friends, but I just never really figured it out.

Daddy loved him some Lizzie more than he cared for me. Mama, well I reckon I didn't really know what mama was thinking. She kept me close and never fussed on Lizzie like daddy did but sometimes I'll catch her brushing Lizzie's hair while she slept and rubbing her forehead; don't remember her ever doing that with me.

Lizzie had all these big dreams and big ideas. She wanted to be some big-time something or the other. Mama never paid it no mind. But daddy, he egged her on every chance he got. One day, Lizzie came running in the house about some class trip to New York. She wanted mama and daddy to pay for her to go on. Mama said no. She thought that we girls shouldn't be off in the world somewhere all alone. Daddy thought Lizzie should go.

"She'll get to see something more than just Arbor," daddy said.

But mama didn't care and when mama said no, it was no. What she lacked in height and weight, she made up for in mean. Guess that's why Mr. Atkins always said that Mama was a mean somebody. People around Arbor would think twice before starting any mess with her. She had all these crazy evil nicknames at the hospital where she worked as a nurse. No one dared disobey mama, not even daddy. So, when she said Lizzie wasn't going, Lizzie wasn't going.

We were all sitting in the living room when mama forbade Lizzie from going. When Mama left the room, daddy gave Lizzie a long hug. I walked away cause I didn't feel bad at all for her. Something didn't let me walk far. I stood around the corner and listened. Lizzie was crying when daddy let her go. She didn't understand why mama was being so harsh. Daddy wiped her tears and kissed her forehead.

"It will be alright princess," daddy said.

"I just want to go see the lights daddy," Lizzie said.

"One day you will Lizzie," daddy said.

He hugged her again and rubbed her hair gently. Daddy thought Lizzie was going to be someone important one day; that she would get out of Arbor and be great.

I watched them and wondered why he didn't think that of me. What made him so sure that Lizzie would get out of Arbor and not me? What was so different about Lizzie?

I walked away leaving them there and found mama in the backyard tending to her garden. I knelt down next to her to help.

"Mama," I said.

"What child?" mama replied.

"Do you think we will ever leave Arbor?" I asked.

"Why would you want to leave Arbor?" mama asked.

"Because daddy said there's a big world out there, we should be a part of it," I answered.

"Your daddy talks nonsense. Ain't no place better than Arbor," mama said.

"But daddy seem to think so. He seems to think that Lizzie –"

"Odessa, your daddy don't know nothing about nothing. You or Lizzie ain't bout to go nowhere."

Mama's voice was stern and cold. I know she meant what she was saying. Mama wasn't like daddy, she didn't encourage day dreams. We were born in Arbor and we were gonna stay in Arbor. I knew that and somewhere deep down Lizzie had to have known that as well.

I lifted my head and saw Lizzie sitting on the porch swing reading that silly book she done read over a hundred times. A smile came across her face, and her eyes got all glass and started to wonder. Life for Lizzie was all kinds of roses. She just saw things bigger and better. It always seemed to her like things were more than what the human eyes could see. Like she had these special gifts that made the world bright and beautiful.

I reckon that was why folks just loved her. She made them feel special; she gave them hope. When Lizzie talked, folks listened. When I talked, it was like my mouth was moving but no sound came out.

I wondered what was it about Lizzie that made everyone care so much. I didn't hate her, not at all, I just wanted to know why folks saw her but they never saw me. Watching Lizzie sitting on the porch swing, I decided that I was going to be her shadow. I was going to follow her wherever she went and listen to every word she said. I had to know why Lizzie was so special and I wasn't. It sounds crazy now. But the moment Lizzie was born, I became invisible, and I just wanted to know why.

32

The next day at school I started to follow Lizzie. I didn't want her to know what I was up to, so I kept my distance. It wasn't too hard, most folk never even realize I was ever in the room, it was like they saw right through me; even Lizzie.

I skipped class to spy on her cheerleading practice. She looked like some sort of model or something in her cheerleading outfit. I looked down at my dark, dreary clothes I was wearing and realized one thing; one of the reasons people liked Lizzie was because she was beautiful. I wasn't.

I sat way up on the bleachers and watched as Lizzie and the rest of the squad went over their routine. Lizzie kept them in control. She took charge, and they all listened to her. I sat alone. No one listened to me; no one followed my lead.

I turned my head slightly to see who else was around and then my eyes landed on Randel who was sitting further down the bleachers to the right of me. I don't think he knew

I was there. He had a book opened as if he was reading but it looked more like he was watching the same thing I was watching.

For a moment, I stopped watching Lizzie and started watching Randel. I think I loved Randel from the moment I met him. I always thought that Randel and I would one day be back to what we were, maybe even more. But it was our senior year, and just like everyone else, Randel saw right through me.

The thing was, I think Randel saw through most folk. He always stayed to himself reading and studying, that's how I knew that if anybody was going to make it out of Arbor, Randel would. I got up and walked down to where Randel was sitting and sat down next to him, but he didn't realize I was there. His mind was lost in whatever it was that he was looking at.

Lizzie must have finally seen me sitting in the bleachers because she threw her hand in the air and waved at me. But for some reason, Randel must have thought she was waving at him because he waved back with a silly grin on his face.

Lizzie put her hand down and gave him a crazy look. Then she pointed at me. Randel turned his head and looked at me with his face filled with embarrassment. Lizzie grinned and went back to practicing.

"Oh. Hey Odessa," Randel said as he turned his head and pretended to read his book.

"Hey Randel. What're you reading?" I asked.

"Just some math stuff," he replied.

"Oh," I said trying to think of something else I could say. "So, thinking of going to prom?"

"Hadn't really thought about it. Besides, I think it's way too soon," he said.

"Oh yeah, I think so too. I was just asking," I replied.

I sat back on the bleachers and watched Lizzie again. I noticed that her attention was on the guys on the football team as they practiced. I couldn't figure out who she was looking at, but whoever it was she sure was into him.

"Hey Odessa." Randel's voice calling my name was like romance music playing softly in my ear. I could hear him call my name all day.

I sat up straight. "Yeah."

"Do you think… you know what, don't worry about it." Randel got up and put his book in his book bag and then placed his book bag on his shoulder. "I'll see you around," Randel said as he walked away.

I wondered what Randel was going to ask me. I felt like running after him and asking him what he wanted, but by then, Lizzie was done with her practice and making her way to the girl's locker room.

I followed and sat in the back of the locker room behind a bunch of lockers and just listened. There were a whole lot of giggling and laughing. They all acted like they were the center of the universe, like nothing could touch them, as if they were better than anybody else. Of course, Lizzie was their queen.

"Hey are you guys going to the woods tonight?" one of the girls asked.

"I am, but Lizzie may have special plans for her man tonight," Cecilia said with a chuckle.

All the other girls said, "Awwwwww!" and giggled hysterically.

I sat up and listened closely because that was the first time I heard of Lizzie having a boyfriend.

"Will y'all cut it out?" Lizzie replied with a grin.

"Ken and black Barbie," Cecilia said prompting the other girls to bust out laughing.

Lizzie picked up a towel and threw it at them and then went into the shower. I waiting, listening intensely for them to say who Lizzie's boyfriend was but they changed the subject. I thought back to the way Lizzie was watching the football team practiced, and I realized that it may be one of them. But there was like a hundred guys on the football team, and I didn't know where to even start. Lizzie had a boyfriend, and I didn't know why it mattered to me so much, but I had to find out who he was.

33

After school, I followed Lizzie and her friends to the dinner. They must have giggled the entire way there and of course didn't none of them see me walking closely behind them.

As we approached the diner, I saw Randel standing there. That crazy Brady Hatcher was messing with him. He kept slapping Randel's books out of his hand and every time he tried to pick it up Brady would push him down.

Lizzie's friends walked by slowly looking as if they wanted to say something but couldn't. Brady was mean and a troublemaker. He always comes around with his no-good friends just to cause trouble and didn't nobody want any parts of that.

Nobody except Lizzie. She got right in between Randel and Brady daring Brady to touch Randel again. Randel was on the ground looking up at Lizzie like a lost puppy dog. I could see the anger building up in Brady's face cause his whole face turned blood red. I looked around in a panic cause I just knew Brady was about to do something Lizzie and Randel were too afraid to help. My heart was in my thought.

But just as Brady violently grabbed hold of Lizzie's arm, the whole football team came out of nowhere, and Caleb Roberts grabbed hold of Brady's collar and wasn't about to let go. He pushed Brady away from Lizzie and Randel. One of Caleb's friends had to get Caleb off Brady. You think that crazy Brady would have ended it there. He wanted to take on the whole football team right then and there.

If Sheriff Roberts, Caleb's dad, hadn't shown up, it probably would have been a big old mess of a fight.

"What's going on here boys?" Sheriff Robert said.

"Brady over here causing problems daddy," Caleb said.

Brady gave Caleb the meanest look ever. But Caleb didn't back down. He stared down Brady like he was waiting for him to do something.

"Is that true Brady?" Sheriff Roberts asked.

"No, everything's alright Sheriff," Brady answered.

"I hope so. Why don't you get out of here," Sheriff Roberts said.

Brady turned to leave but not before he gave Randel and Lizzie the coldest look ever. It sent chills down my spine. Must have sent chills down Lizzie's spine as well because she grabbed hold of Caleb's arm and tried to hide behind him and the rest of the football team. That was the first time I think I ever saw Lizzie scared.

"Randel you doing alright son?" Sheriff Roberts asked after Brady had walked away.

Randel stood up slowly nodding his head yes. He looked over at Lizzie, and I could tell he felt a bit embarrassed. Randel wasn't the big tough guy, but it must have been a real blow to his ego for Lizzie to have to come to his rescue.

"Alright, then you kids go on ahead now," Sheriff Roberts said as he patted Caleb on the shoulders.

The football team all walked into the dinner where the cheerleading squad were watching everything go down from the window. Caleb waited for Lizzie while she went on and helped Randel pick up his books from the floor before she went into the ice cream parlor. I went over to Randel as he watched Caleb and Lizzie walk away.

"Are you ok?" I asked Randel.

"I hate that she had to see that," he said.

"What did Brady want from you?" I asked.

"Nothing, just always mess with me, since we were kids," Randel answered.

"What an ass," I replied.

"You think she'll think bad of me after this?" Randel asked.

"Who?" I responded.

"Lizzie," he answered. "You think she'll think I was weak or something?"

"I don't know. Why?" I replied.

"Just wondering. I don't want her to think I can't do what Caleb did," he said.

"You're not Caleb, Randel. I for one think you're better than Caleb and all those boys on the football team," I told him.

"But what do you think she would think?" he asked again.

"What does it matter?" I replied.

"I don't know; it just mattered to me what she thinks," he said.

I looked at Randel and my heart sunk because that's when I realized that Randel loved Lizzie. I watched as he walked away and streams of tears fell down my face. I'd loved Randel since kindergarten, but he loved Lizzie. He cared what Lizzie thought about him, how Lizzie felt.

I looked through the window at Lizzie and all her friends giggling and having a great time while I stood on the outside with tears flowing down my face. Lizzie had it all, even Randel's heart, the only thing I wanted.

34

It had been a few days since I started following Lizzie and other than making myself sick with annoyance at how everyone, especially Randel, gushed over her, there was nothing to find. She went to school every day, then to cheerleading practice, then to the diner, then every night she'd sneak out of the house to go and meet all her friends in them woods.

Them woods were the hot spot for all the cool kids like Lizzie. They get there and play music and laugh like they ain't had a care in the world. I use to sit in a special spot behind some rocks and bushes just watching and listening. As usual, no one ever saw me there. I'd just sit there and watch. That's how I found out who Lizzie's boyfriend was.

It was a clear summer's night, and the breeze blew across the leaves softly and would whisper gently in my ears. I sat in my special spot, and I watched as they danced in the moonlight away from all the others. Lizzie's face lighted up and glowed as he touched her. Their bodies fit together perfectly, and they basically melted in each other's arms.

He was the most popular boy in school, so why wouldn't he be head-over-heels in love with Lizzie. I moved in closer to try and hear what they were saying. He held on tightly to Lizzie and looked deeply into her eyes.

"You're bout the most beautiful girl I have ever seen Elizabeth Potter," he said to Lizzie.

"Well, ain't you the charmer Caleb Roberts?" Lizzie said.

Caleb smiled at Lizzie stroking her face gently. They looked like one of them couples from one of Lizzie's stupid romance novels. It was obvious from Caleb's eyes that Lizzie was his whole world. I ain't never had a man look at me the way Caleb looked at Lizzie, ever.

I just sat there and watched them dance. They danced even when the music had gone off, and most everyone had gone home. If Cecilia hadn't come to break them up, they might have danced the whole night.

Caleb walked Lizzie and Cecilia out the woods to our house then he gave Lizzie the sweetest kiss I'd ever seen.

Then he walked away as Cecilia and Lizzie giggled and gushed over him. They stood in the back yard for a moment and started talking. I hid behind a nearby tree just to listen.

"You guys are perfect together," Cecilia said.

"I know I can't believe how amazing he is," Lizzie said with stars in her eyes.

"So, when are you going to tell him?" Cecilia asked.

"I don't know," Lizzie said with a worried look on her face. "What if he hates me after he finds out?"

"Caleb's not going to hate you. He's the best guy ever. He'll make everything alright. I'm sure of it," Cecilia said.

"I don't know Cecilia," Lizzie said.

"Trust me Lizzie, it'll be alright," Cecilia said. "Let me go before my dad wake up and notice I'm gone. You don't want to get your mama after you either."

Cecilia hugged Lizzie and then ran off. Lizzie went back to the house the same way she came out, through the basement window. I walked out from behind the tree where

I was hiding and wondered what them two were talking about.

Although Lizzie and I were sisters, we didn't share our innermost secrets. Lizzie had Cecilia for that, and I had, well, I just kept it to myself. I caught myself feeling kinda hurt that Lizzie shared so much with Cecilia. But then, as if the devil had risen up in me, I grew angry. I was angry that Lizzie had a friend to share all her secrets with, I was angry that she had secrets, I was angry that she had friends at all that she could sneak out of the house and meet just to hang out, but most of all I was angry that Lizzie had love. She was loved by Caleb and she was loved by Randel.

I wanted to be loved by Randel. I realized for the first time that I hated my sister. I hated everything about her, and I just wanted her to go away. Far away from me, far away from Randel. I had to make Lizzie go away, no matter what it took.

35

The next morning, I woke up pissed at myself for having thoughts of wanting my sister to go away. How could I think like that? How could I have allowed my mind to go there? What was wrong with me? I started to feel so guilty. I knew that I had to figure out a way to get over this hatred for my sister. It took me a long time to even admit that I hated her.

If folks knew, they would think I was just jealous. But I dared anyone to live with someone who was so damn perfect. Nothing they did was ever wrong. I wasn't Odessa, I was Lizzie's sister, and that's all I was ever going to be.

I laid on my bed and covered my eyes with my hands. I imagined being the pretty one, the one who everyone loved; the one who Randel loved. I smiled to myself at the thought of how Lizzie would feel being me. Being the girl who everyone turned their backs on. If only daddy could see that his precious princess wasn't so perfect, if only they all could see that about Lizzie.

I could hear mama and daddy arguing again downstairs. It seemed to be an everyday thing now. I took the pillow and covered my face to drown out the sound of their voices. Then Lizzie came into my room.

"Hey Odessa," she said, "they going at it again."

"Yeah, I hear them," I responded while taking the pillow off my face and sitting up in the bed.

Lizzie closed my bedroom door and walked around my room as if she was searching for something. Her face seemed to wonder, and her eyes landed on every single wall in my room.

"Did you want something Lizzie?" I asked her.

"Not really. You know my room's right above the kitchen, and that's where they're doing their latest episode of who hates who more," Lizzie replied. "I wish daddy would get the strength to leave here."

"What? You sound crazy Lizzie," I replied.

"You don't even see it, do you Odessa?" Lizzie said.

"See what?" I asked

"Daddy's drowning here. He and mama ain't happy," Lizzie answered.

"So that means he should leave. Where is he going to go?" I said.

"If it means that he's going to be happy, I don't care where he goes," Lizzie said.

"So you want our daddy to just up and leave us?" I asked.

"I'm not saying he should up and leave, but listen to them Odessa, they ain't happy, and there's too much happiness in the world to be stuck someplace where you ain't happy. Folks need to be free to follow what they want," Lizzie explained.

"You're talking crazy Lizzie. Folks can't just follow what they want, especially daddy. There's something called responsibilities," I told her.

"Why can't folks follow what they want and still be responsible? You want to hang with me, and my friends don't you?" Lizzie asked with smirk.

"What are you talking about?" I sat up straight and looked at her.

"Well, ain't that why you been following us around the past few days? I mean I don't know why you just didn't come on and join us. I swear Odessa if I didn't know you any better I swear you were one of them crazy people," Lizzie told me.

I sat on my bed in shock as I looked at Lizzie fixing her hair in my mirror. I hadn't realized that Lizzie had noticed me. I thought for sure that she hadn't seen me, I mean between all her giggling and carrying on with her friends, I figured I'd be the last thing on her radar.

"Why didn't you say anything if you saw me?" I asked softly.

"Well, I figured you weren't ready just yet," Lizzie replied.

"Ready for what?" I asked.

"Ready to stop hiding in the shadows. I just don't understand you Odessa, why are you so comfortable being a nobody?" Lizzie listened at the door, "Man, I don't think they're ever going to stop. I think I'm going to go to my me place and block them out. I'm so tired of their fussing."

Lizzie's "me place" was what she called her hiding place. A place she would go to be alone and read her books. She said it made her feel high above the world, as if she was untouchable.

Lizzie left the room, and I slammed the door behind her. How dare she think I was comfortable being a nobody? If only she knew what it was like having people look at you like you were nothing, like you didn't matter?

I walked over to the mirror and looked at my reflections. Tears flowed down my face, and my eyes were about to turn red. It was in that moment that I realized what needed to be done. Lizzie had to know what it was like to be me and have people hate her and I knew exactly what I had to do to make that happen.

36

That night, I went to the football game. It was so packed with people. Those damn games were all we had in Arbor. It was all folks looked forward to. I sat there and watched Lizzie and her friends do their cheers and get the crowd all hyped up. Just watching Lizzie got me even angrier. The only pleasure I had to console me was that she was going to get hers soon.

I just knew that my plan to make Lizzie see what it was like to be invisible and ignored by people was going to work. It was past time Lizzie got what was coming to her.

I left the game right before it ended and went back to the house. It actually took me a few moments to get up the nerves to put my plan into action. I was pacing up and down my room for a while until finally, I had to do it.

I picked the phone and dialed. The moment Randel's voice came on the other end, my body froze. I couldn't speak. There was such a delicate and sweet tone to his voice that I caught myself blushing a little.

"Hello? Who's this?" Randel asked.

"Hey Randel it's me Odessa," I finally said.

"Oh, hey Odessa. What's up?" replied Randel.

"I need your help. Well not me really but Lizzie," I responded.

"Why… what's wrong with Lizzie?" Randel asked in a panic voice.

"I overheard some guys talking about doing something to her tonight in the woods," I said trying to sound scared.

"What? Who?" Randel asked.

"Caleb Roberts and some of his friends. I didn't know what to do," I answered.

"Are they there now?" Randel asked.

"Yeah, I think so. Randel, you need to get there. Tell Caleb that you're her boyfriend and he needs to back off. Please Randel, I don't want him hurting my sister."

"Ok, I'm on my way there now." Randel hung up the phone.

I was giddy with joy. The moment Randel tells Caleb that he's Lizzie's boyfriend, Caleb would think that Lizzie's been cheating on him. Then he would have no other choice but to dump her and hate her forever and all of Lizzie's perfect friends would hate her for treating Caleb that way. As for Randel, well Lizzie would hate him, and if I knew my sister, she would have no problem telling him that. Maybe that's just what he needed to get her out of his system.

I was so excited to see all this go down that I quickly made my way to the woods. But by the time I got there, it seems like a lot of commotion had happened. I could hear people yelling and carrying on, but before I could get close enough to see what had happened, I saw Lizzie and Caleb running coming towards me. I quickly jumped behind the bushes and hid.

They stopped a few feet in front of where I was hiding. Caleb grabbed hold of Lizzie and gave her hug.

"Are you ok?" he asked her.

"Yeah, I think so," Lizzie replied.

"Good. Ok, go home. I need to go back and see what mess Brady and his friends made," Caleb said.

"No Caleb. What if you get hurt what are we going to do?" Lizzie said placing her hand on her stomach.

Caleb placed his hand over hers and smiled. "Ain't nothing going to happen. We're going to be alright."

"We need to get out of here," Lizzie said.

"I know, that's why I said for you to go home," Caleb replied.

"No, I mean we need to get out of Arbor," Lizzie said.

"What? Why?" Caleb asked.

"We need to be someplace where the Brady's of the world don't exist. Someplace that's just for us," Lizzie answered.

"That's crazy Lizzie, this is our home. This is where our family is," Caleb replied.

"But we're starting our own family Caleb," Lizzie said. "I thought you said we would leave. I got all packed."

"I know Lizzie, but I just don't think it's a good idea. We need our family now," Caleb replied.

Just then I realized Lizzie's secret. She was pregnant. My sister was going to have a baby. For the first time, I took the time to really look at my sister's face, she looked scared. All the perfection that I thought was there was gone, and it was just my little sister who was pregnant and scared. I wanted to come from behind the bushes and give her a hug, but before I could do anything, Randel came storming up.

He jumped on Caleb and pushed him to the ground. Caleb had some size on Randel but Randel surprised him, and he wasn't ready for it. But Caleb got up with anger and yelled, "What's your problem?" shoving Randel back.

Randel shoved Caleb again, but this time Caleb didn't fall. Randel yelled, "Stay away from her! You hear me! Stay away!"

Caleb and Lizzie were confused. Randel's eyes were different; it was like something else had taken hold of him.

"I don't know what the hell is wrong with you, but you better get on out of here," Caleb said as anger started to set in.

Randel grabbed hold of Lizzie's arm and tried to pull her towards him. Caleb reached for him and tried to get him off Lizzie. Caleb and Randel started to fight, and I could hear Lizzie yell, "Stop! Stop!"

But they just kept on exchanging blows. At one point Randel got the strength from God only knows where and flipped Caleb on his back on the ground. Then Randel got on top of him and started hitting Caleb something crazy.

"Get off him! Caleb!" Lizzie yelled. But Randel was like a wild animal.

Blood was coming from Caleb's mouth and face, but he couldn't do nothing to get a hold of Randel. I was frozen in place. I didn't know what to do.

Then it happened. Randel went down on the ground with his eyes wide open, but he wasn't moving. My eyes landed on Caleb who was looking at Randel in shock.

Then we both looked up at Lizzie who was standing over Randel's body holding a large rock that was stained by

Randel's blood. She was looking down at Randel's body. Her face was like stone. Her eyes were almost popping out of her head. Her mouth was opened, but there was no sound coming out.

My hands were shaking. I used them to cover up my mouth to keep from screaming. But my whole body shook like a leaf, and I didn't know how much longer I could keep in my scream.

Caleb rushed to his feet and took the rock off Lizzie's hand and threw it to the ground. He looked her over to make sure she was alright, but she still said nothing. Caleb went over to Randel and checked his pulse. He then looked up at Lizzie and said, "He's dead."

Just then my scream came roaring out of me. I couldn't hold it in any longer. Randel was dead, and Lizzie killed him.

Caleb came to the bushes where I was hiding and got me out. "Odessa stop," Caleb said trying to calm me down.

I looked over at Lizzie, and she was standing there staring at Randel's body like a ghost, not moving, not talking. Caleb looked around, but it was just us there. He walked me over to where Lizzie was standing and said, "Stay with Lizzie, I'm going to get help."

I nodded my head and put my arms around Lizzie; she was stiff. Caleb took off running out of the woods. I turned to look at Lizzie, but she wouldn't move. Then I heard someone coming and I wanted to run but I couldn't leave Lizzie.

The trees parted and there stood my daddy. I ran up to him and jumped in his arms. He looked at me confused and then at Lizzie and then at Randel's dead body.

"What happened?" my daddy asked.

"Lizzie," I said softly.

"Lizzie what?" he asked.

"I think Lizzie killed Randel," I said quietly.

My daddy ran to Randel to feel his pulse, and then he got up and scooped up Lizzie in his arms. "We got to get out of here," he said.

I didn't want to leave Randel like that by himself all alone in the woods. I told my daddy that I had to go and get someone to see about Randel. He agreed and took off with Lizzie in his arms.

I sat curled up on the rocks across from Randel's body. I felt so ashamed of what I had done. It was all my fault. Randel wouldn't have been in the woods if it wasn't for me trying to get back at Lizzie.

My eyes landed on the bloody rock that Lizzie used to hit Randel. I got up and picked it up. I walked over to the edge of the cliff and threw it into the river. I fell to my knees and in agony screamed "NO! NO!"

Just then Caleb and his dad, Sheriff Roberts, came up. Caleb ran over to me as he looked around.

"Odessa, where's Lizzie? Where's Lizzie Odessa?" Caleb asked in a panic.

My eyes were glued to the bottom of the cliff, and I couldn't find the words. Caleb must have thought that my agony was because Lizzie had jumped because he too tried to jump over the cliff screaming Lizzie's name. His daddy had to get a hold of him quick.

Sheriff Roberts stood the two of us up straight and looked us in the eyes.

"Now you two listen to me. No one is going to know what happened here or that the two of you were here. I'm going to investigate this as if someone killed Randel and Lizzie is missing. You two don't say nothing to no one about this night. Do you two hear me?" he said to us.

Caleb and I both nodded yes. I don't know what Caleb told his dad about what happened that night and I never asked. I reckoned Sheriff Roberts thought he was protecting Caleb somehow. Caleb and I wanted to protect Lizzie, so we did what Sheriff Roberts asked.

When I got back to the house, I told my mama and daddy what Sheriff Roberts said. I also told them that both Caleb and Sheriff Roberts thought Lizzie had jumped over the cliff. My mama's eyes lit up.

"That's good," she said.

"What?" my daddy asked.

"If they think she dead Henry then that means they can't put her in jail for murder," my mama said.

"How is she going to be dead when she's right here?" My daddy asked.

"Well, we just gonna have to make her invisible to the world for as long as possible," my mama said.

I looked at Lizzie sitting in the chair without emotion and without a voice. I had gotten what I wanted. Lizzie was invisible.

37

Sheriff Roberts stayed true to his word. He made it seem like Lizzie had gone missing and Brady and his friends were to blame. The whole town was out looking for her. Caleb acting like he was searching too but he would always end up at the edge of the cliff just looking over it, like he was waiting for Lizzie to come up from under the water and run into his arms. Mama played her part of the grieving mother and made me do the same. Daddy refused. Mama told folks that he wasn't in his right mind. Folks knew how much daddy loved Lizzie, so they didn't ask any questions.

We kept Lizzie hidden in the house for a couple of days until the search had died down. Then mama went about finding someplace to hide her. I couldn't leave her side. I stayed with her all day and slept in her room. I bathed her, brushed her hair, and changed her clothes.

One day, while she was looking out of the window, she lifted her head slightly and looked at me. I thought for sure she was coming out of whatever hole her mind had gone into, but her eyes were still empty. I grabbed her hand and cried.

"I'm so sorry Lizzie," I said to her. "This is all my fault. I promise you, I'll always take care of you."

She didn't even blink. She just stared back out of the window. I knew that what I had done had made my sister lost to us. Even the town wasn't like it once was. Most folks thought that Brady and his friends had done something to Lizzie and killed Randel. For the first time since I could remember, everyone was conscious of race. Black folks started to leave; they didn't feel safe here anymore. White folks stayed to themselves. No one smiled as much, even when they did, it didn't seem genuine.

I did that. I'd changed an entire town. I had to live with that. The guilt was heavy. But it wasn't nothing compared to seeing mama and daddy's face when I told them that Lizzie was pregnant.

"What do you mean she's pregnant?" mama asked as she went over to Lizzie who was laying on her back in the bed, and felt on her stomach.

"Lizzie can't be pregnant," daddy said.

"She is. I heard her say it that night," I explained.

"Oh my God!" daddy proclaimed.

"Who's the father?" mama asked.

"Caleb Roberts," I answered.

"Caleb!" mama yelled.

Daddy sat on the chair across from Lizzie and it looked like everything he held close to him had been destroyed. His eyes welled up with tears and he buried his face in his hands.

Mama paced around the room thinking. "If we tried to get rid of the baby then people will know that Lizzie is alive. Besides, it's against God," she said seeming to be talking to herself.

Daddy finally stood up and walked out of the room. He didn't look any of us in the eyes. I don't remember daddy ever looking any of us in the eyes after that.

"I know a place," mama blurted out.

"Where?" I asked.

"There's an abandoned cabin on the other side of the woods. We'll take her there and leave her there until she has the baby," mama explained.

That's exactly what we did. I never left the cabin. Mama would go and come. She didn't want folks thinking something was wrong and come snooping around. When they asked for me, she said that I was deeply depressed and needed time. Daddy never came to the cabin.

The day Lizzie went into labor I didn't know what mama was going to do. I remember it so clearly. The only way we knew something was wrong was because that whole day Lizzie's face kept jerking. I was hoping she was coming back to us, but mama knew.

She left and returned with some guy. I got scared because no one had seen Lizzie alive since that night in the woods. But mama said the man was a doctor from two towns over who owed her a favor. She swore him to secrecy.

The doctor said that Lizzie wouldn't be able to push in her current state so he would have to cut her open. He begged mama to let him take Lizzie to the hospital, but mama refused. She said that the two of them could do it right there in that dirty old cabin. They did just that.

The baby was born so perfect and beautiful, just like Lizzie. I knew she had to go. She had to be away from me before I do the same to her like I did to Lizzie. Mama knew we couldn't keep the baby either. She had a birth certificate from the hospital where she worked and filled it out. She figured that with a birth certificate they could put the baby up for adoption and no one would ask a lot of questions. The only thing she got stuck on was what to name the baby.

I saw Lizzie's favorite book laying on the table by the bed. I had taken to reading it to her from time to time. I remember that the main character's name was Emilia. Mama thought it was pretty enough. I remember picking up the baby and holding her close to my chest and saying, "Welcome to the world Emilia."

I think she smiled at me a little. But all I saw when I looked at the baby was Lizzie, so I put her down and didn't look at her again. Not Even later that night when mama came into the cabin and wrapped the baby up and told me to take her down a path leading to the other town where my daddy would be waiting. I handed her over to my daddy and still didn't look at her.

Daddy did. He gently brushed her chin and put her in the car. Before he got in the car and drove off, he turned to me.

"You be good Odessa," daddy said without looking me in the eye.

I smiled and waved, not realizing that was the last time I would see my daddy. I hated him for leaving us. Mama and I were left to take care of Lizzie all alone, and after mama died it was just me. What was weird was that Lizzie became the only person that I could ever talk to. She was all I had, and she needed me. It was just us and only us.

Part IV

Lizzie

38

When Odessa was done talking, it was as if time stood still. No one knew what to do or say. Chanel looked over at Emilia, but her eyes were locked on Sheriff Caleb Roberts and his eyes on her. Tears streamed down her face as she stared into the eyes of her father. For years she had wondered what it would be like to find her biological father. What would she do or say?

There was so much happening in the moment that Emilia didn't know how to process all that she had heard. All she could do was stare. Her eyes drew lines between every feature on his face. She subliminally placed her face onto his to see if they matched. Her heart grew full of the thought of finally having a father.

Sheriff Caleb walked up to her and gently rubbed his hand across her face. With tears in his eyes, he turned to face Odessa.

"How could ya'll do this?" he asked.

"I'm sorry Caleb. But we had to protect Lizzie," Odessa said.

"I was protecting Lizzie!" he shouted, "my dad did all that because I told him that I killed Randel and Lizzie saw it. I would have taken the blame, not her. I never would have let her take the blame. Why couldn't you guys have trusted that?"

"My parents didn't know that, I didn't know that," Odessa said.

"So you made me believe that she was dead. That my baby was dead. Why would you do that? How cruel could you be?" he replied. "I thought you and I were in this together, that we were protecting Lizzie's secret."

"I didn't mean to hurt you, Caleb. But when you assumed that Lizzie jumped into the river it just seemed… I don't know. I'm sorry," Odessa responded.

He walked over to a tree near where Randel's body was found and sat down. "I lost everything that night Odessa. I blamed myself for a long time. But it was all you," he told her.

"Caleb I'm sorry that you got hurt. But I had to take care of my sister and I ain't gonna apologize for that," Odessa said.

"Where is she?" Emilia asked softly.

Everyone focused their eyes on Odessa and anxiously awaited her response. Odessa looked around at each of them almost in a panic and then back at Emilia.

"She died," Odessa answered.

"You're lying," Emilia said.

"Why would I lie about that?" Odessa asked with a slight smirk.

"For the same reason you've been hiding her for so long, to keep her with you, under your control." Emilia said as she slowly walked up to Odessa.

"Girl you're crazy," Odessa replied.

Sheriff Caleb quickly stood to his feet and looked sternly at Odessa. "Where is she Odessa?"

"I said she died," Odessa said daringly.

Emilia's mind frantically begun to wonder, then suddenly it was like a lightbulb had gone off in her head. "You're such a liar Odessa!" Emilia shouted then she took off running down the trail leading to Odessa's house.

The others follow but could barely keep up with Emilia. She got to the house and up the stairs to the back door. It was locked. Emilia took a flower pot and threw it at the glass on the door. She reached her hand through the broken glass and unlocked the door. Emelia walked in and looked around, wondering where Odessa would have hidden Lizzie.

Then she remembered what Odessa said, that Lizzie's room was right above the kitchen. Emilia made her way to the stairs and ran up quickly. She got to the door and caught her breath before going in.

Emilia turned the door knob and opened it. The room was empty. Emilia looked around the room opening the closet doors and looking under the bed frantically. She just knew Lizzie had to be there. She ran out of the room and met the others at the top of the stairs. She walked up to Odessa in anger, "Where is she?!"

"I told you she died," Odessa answered. "You got what you came for. You know the truth. Just leave and get out of our lives."

"You're lying," Emilia said with her fingers pointed in Odessa's faces.

She, Sheriff Caleb, and Chanel ran through every room upstairs while Sam and Donavan did the same downstairs. But there was no sign of Lizzie. They met up with Odessa in the living room.

"Odessa, you owe me the truth," Sheriff Caleb said.

"I told you the truth Caleb," Odessa said in a calm tone.

"We have to be missing something," Emilia said as her eyes surfed the room.

"There was a place that Odessa talked about that Lizzie called her me place," Sam said. "Sheriff do you know what that place was?"

"She never told me about it," Sheriff Caleb answered.

"You're right Sam," Emilia said. "It's a place where Lizzie felt like she was high above everything. The Attic!"

They all ran back upstairs with Odessa screaming for them to leave her house. When they got to the top of the stairs, they looked up and saw a small door with a drawstring hanging from it. Donavan pulled on the drawstring, and a flight of stairs came down. Emilia led the way up to the attic.

It was fixed perfectly neat. With shelves of books and decorated in beautiful white drapes. There was a bed that was made neatly with lots of plush pillows and one window with beautiful silk curtains. The curtains were open, and the window overlooked the woods. By the window was a rocking chair and in the rocking chair was Lizzie.

She had a clear view of the woods, and she sat there staring out of the window, as if she had been watching them the entire time. Lizzie seemed peaceful, almost like she was just relaxing by the window enjoying the cool afternoon air. Her wavy hair laid neatly down to her shoulders, and her dust-brown skin glowed in her all-white night gown. Her face glued to the window and her eyes glazed into the distance.

Emilia walked up to Lizzie and stood a foot away, too afraid to get any closer. She allowed her eyes to examine her mother's face like she had done with her father's. Finally, Emilia could see herself in someone else. Everything about Lizzie felt like home to Emilia. The vision of her mother overwhelmed Emilia, and she was frozen in place.

Sheriff Caleb ran over to Lizzie and knelt down beside her. He stroked her face and lovely called out her name. Lizzie slightly turned her face, but there was no life in her eyes. She stared but it was like there was no one else in the room with her.

"What's wrong with her?" Sheriff Caleb asked.

"I don't know. She's been that way ever since that night," Odessa said.

Sam walked over to Lizzie and knelt down next to Sheriff Caleb. He started to examine Lizzie and tried to get her to follow his figures. Then he called out her name to see if she would respond verbally or through motion. She didn't.

"What's wrong with her Sam?" Emilia asked.

"If I was to guess, I'd say she was Catatonic," Sam said.

"What does that mean?" Sheriff Caleb asked.

"It's neurological, almost like she's asleep while wide awake. But I can't say for sure without further test," Sam explained.

"Can she come out of it?" Emilia asked.

"I don't know. Obviously it was brought on by trauma, but after so many years without treatment for that trauma, it may be too late," Sam said.

Emilia finally walked over to Lizzie. Sam got up, allowing her to kneel down next to Sheriff Caleb. She grabbed hold of Lizzie's hand and squeezed it tightly. Sheriff Caleb placed his arm around Emilia. The three of them were finally together.

39

The news of Lizzie's resurrection spread through Arbor quickly. By the time they got her to the hospital, people had already lined up to see if it was truly her. Sheriff Caleb didn't allow anyone to touch her. He carried Lizzie from the house, into his car, and then carried her through the hospital doors. The pain of joy read across his face. He squeezed her gently in his arms to make sure she was really there. The doctors had to convince him to let her go. Emilia stood by his side as they watch the doctor's lay her on a gurney and roll her into a private room. Sam went along to make sure they administered the proper test.

Cecilia got to the hospital just as they were taking Lizzie away. Her body was shaking with anticipation and fear. Her face wet with tears and her eyes blood red from crying.

"Caleb, is it true?" Celia asked as she stood behind Sheriff Caleb and Emilia.

Sheriff Caleb turned and immediately fell into Cecilia's arms. "Yes, she's came back to us," he told her.

"But how?" Cecilia asked again with confusion on her face.

"Odessa," Emilia answered.

"She was in that house the whole time?" Cecilia asked again as she released Sheriff Caleb from their embrace.

"Yeah. Odessa had her locked in the cellar," he answered.

"I've been by that house thousands of times. I figured Lizzie would have wanted me to check on Odessa, no matter how mean she had gotten. But never once did I…. Oh God if I had known." Cecilia covered her face with her hands, and Sheriff Caleb wrapped his hands around her.

"Don't blame yourself, Cecilia. We all thought she was dead," he said.

"But she's not," Emilia said placing her hand softly on Cecilia's back.

Cecilia lifted her head to look at Emilia. She finally allowed herself to see Lizzie in Emilia. She ran her fingers across Emilia's face.

"If I hadn't been so stubborn I would have seen it. Everything beautiful in Lizzy is in you. You're your mother's child," Cecilia said.

Emilia smiled to herself and wiped away the tears from her eyes. When she turned her head, she saw Randel's sister, Olive, walk in. Emilia excused herself and went up to her.

"So is it true? Is Lizzie alive?" Olive asked her.

"Yes, she is," Emilia answered.

"Did she tell you what happened to my brother?" Olive asked again.

"She can't speak. She doesn't even know where she is," Emilia answered.

"Oh," Olive said looking disappointed.

"But I do know what happened in the woods that night," Emilia said.

Olive looked up with relief. Emilia sat Olive down and explained everything to her. She told the story just as Odessa had told it to her. Then she watched the expression on Olives face. She thought Olive would be angry. That she would demand justice for her brother. But Olive almost seemed relieved. She had been waiting for answers for so long that now that was all that mattered.

Olive looked up at Emilia and asked, "Is Lizzie going to be alright?"

"I don't know. She's been locked away for so long, never receiving the help that she needed. She may never come back to us fully. I'm sorry Olive," Emilia explained.

"No. She didn't mean to kill him. My brother loved her, and he would want her to be alright." Olive stood up and looked back at Emilia, "Thank you for giving me closure and helping my brother to finally rest in peace."

Olive left Emilia sitting there wondering what to do next. She had gone on this journey to find her mother, and now that she'd found her, she didn't know what she was supposed to do. Emilia leaned her head back against the wall and took a deep breath.

40

Odessa sat on her back porch and somberly stared at the woods in the distance. She wrapped her arms around her waist and allowed her body to go numb. The wind gently ran across her face, but she couldn't feel anything. The loneliness that she had been in her whole life had suddenly overwhelmed her and became even more unbearable. Everyone was gone, and she had nothing left.

"Odessa," A male voice called from behind her.

Odessa slowly turned to see Sam standing behind her. For the first time, Odessa actually took the time to look at him; he resembled their father, Henry. Odessa quickly turned back to look at the woods. Not being able to bear seeing Henry's disappointed eyes coming through Sam.

"What do you want now?" Odessa asked angrily.

Sam walked over to her and sat down. He held a large brown envelope tightly in his hand and rubbed on it slightly.

Odessa tried to act as if he wasn't there. But her eyes would glare at him from the side.

"I just wanted to check on you," Sam replied.

"Well, I'm fine. So now you can leave," Odessa replied.

"I don't think I can do that," Sam replied as he turned to look at her.

"And why the hell not?" Odessa asked sternly.

"Because I'm all you got," Sam replied with a warm smile.

Sam's response angered Odessa even more. She didn't want to be reminded of all that she had lost. She stood up and faced Sam.

"I ain't never needed nobody and wasn't nobody ever there for me! I ain't got time to be playing family reunion with you so just go on, get the hell out of here."

Odessa's yells fell on Sam's ears but her pain laid on his heart. He stood up and wrapped his arms around her squeezing her tightly. Sam's unexpected gesture confused

Odessa. She didn't know whether to hug him back or pull away. She chose to pull away.

"What the hell are you doing?" she asked softly.

"I figured you need that," Sam replied.

"Well, you figured wrong. Odessa said as she took a step back.

Sam shook the large brown envelope in his hand and then reached out hand to hand it to her.

"What's this?" she asked him.

"My mother was cleaning out our father's things, and she found these. I didn't go through them because it's all for you," Sam explained.

Odessa took the envelope from Sam and opened it. There were smaller white envelopes tied together with a rubber band, and there were a lot of them. Odessa took out one of the smaller white envelopes and opened it; it was a birthday card addressed to her from Henry.

"It looks like he never forgot your birthday," Sam said.

Odessa looked at him and then back down at the birthday card. Suddenly her legs felt weak, and she had to sit down.

"I destroyed my family," she said in a low voice. "I was so jealous of Lizzie that I destroyed my family."

Sam Knelt down beside his sister and said, "You still have me Odessa."

Odessa looked Sam in the eyes and grabbed hold of his hand. She squeezed it, holding it close to her chest. Tears streamed down her face, and Odessa let out a loud relieving breath.

41

The woods felt peaceful for the first time since Emilia got to Arbor. She stood in the middle of the clearing, the last place Lizzie stood with Caleb, and admired the beauty of the woods. The sky above was clear blue, and the clouds were barely visible. The trees danced along to the gentle breeze and Emilia took it all in.

"I thought I'd find you here," a voice said from behind her.

Emilia turned around to see Sheriff Caleb standing behind her. She smiled like a child at the sight of her father.

"I just wanted to give it one last look I guess," Emilia replied.

"Yeah, me too," Sheriff Caleb said as he looked at Emilia almost seeming too afraid to touch her. "I'm sorry Emilia. I missed a lot with you."

"It wasn't your fault," Emilia said.

"Did you have a good life?" Sheriff Caleb asked.

"Yeah, I did. My adopted mother was the best. She loved me," Emilia answered.

"Well, I guess I thank the good Lord for that," Sheriff Caleb said as he walked passed her and stared into the clearing. "That night we planned on leaving. But I chickened out. I sat up all night wondering what if we had, what if we'd never gone to the game or come to these woods. Life would have been different." Sheriff Caleb turned to face Emilia again. "I would have gotten to be your father."

"So that's why her bag was here with all her things in it. She left it when the fight broke out," Emilia said.

"Yup. Lizzie was ready to go. We planned it all the night before, but I couldn't do it. I couldn't leave. I screwed up everything for us," Sheriff Caleb said with his head lowered.

Emilia got closer to him and grabbed hold of his hand, "You didn't," she said. "It's not too late to be my father. I never had one, and I could sure use one."

Sheriff Caleb squeezed her hand and pulled her close to him. He wrapped his arms around her and embraced her tightly. Tears streamed from both of their eyes, and neither one of them wanted to let go.

Finally, Sheriff Caleb released her but still kept his arms around her.

"So, Sam found this specialist for Lizzie up there in New York. They're supposed to fly her up today," he said.

"Yeah, I plan on flying with her. Will you come?" Emilia replied.

"Absolutely," Sheriff Caleb said.

They gave one another smile and turned to walk out of the woods. Sheriff Caleb laid his arms across Emilia's shoulders, and Emilia wrapped her arms around his waist.

"So, since I'm a father now, how about we talk about this Donavan fella," Sheriff Roberts said, "what exactly are his intentions?"

Emilia let out a loud laughter and held him tighter as they walked off together leaving behind the woods and all of its secrets.

THE END